The
Death
Kiss

The
Death
Kiss

MADELON ST. DENIS

COACHWHIP PUBLICATIONS
GREENVILLE, OHIO

The Author

Very little is known about the author, Madelon St. Denis. The use of 'St. Dennis' on her two traditionally published books appears to be a change by her publisher to accommodate marketing of those titles, as 'St. Denis' was often used on her magazine novels and foreign translations. 'St. Denis' is also how her name appears on a 1930 U.S. Census form, which notes she was born in 1885 in Massachusetts, and had been married at the age of 23. (She was 45 at the time of the census, lodging in New York.) One of her books, *The Death Kiss,* was made into a movie, so her name appears in conjunction with that in the 1930s, but she appears to have stopped writing by the end of the decade.

The Death Kiss, by Madelon St. Denis
© 2024 Coachwhip Publications edition

First published 1932
CoachwhipBooks.com

ISBN 1-61646-590-5
ISBN-13 978-1-61646-590-2

1

Strangled

"Now!" Sydney Traherne's fingers brushed the inspector's sleeve. "Watch the third window from the end, the one with the ornamental balcony."

Thus directed, Inspector Fisk's eyes deserted the parade marching smartly across the screen and traveled upward to the designated window. In it stood an elderly man, alone, his attention apparently fixed on the column of moving figures in the street below, then, as the news reel camera persistently clung to the passing parade the man at the upper window flung out both hands in an oddly startled gesture, and abruptly vanished into the shadowy depths of the room behind him.

The two watching men in the audience moved, preparatory to departure, and, as the news reel commenced another subject, left their seats, neither speaking until they had gained the theater lobby.

"Was I right?" Traherne inquired quietly when they had lighted cigarettes and were making for the side exit nearest his parked car.

Conway Fisk delayed answering until they were settled in his friend's car, threading a slow way through the congested crosstown traffic. "Though at the angle the camera was tilted the man showed indistinctly, I think you're right, it looked as if he fell, rather than stepped back."

Traherne nodded briefly. "Recognize the building?"

"No."

"It's the Stanwix Bank and Trust. Why not drive over and take a look at it? I couldn't catch the name on that third window."

"Very well," the inspector rather half-heartedly agreed, adding a second or two later: "How'd you happen to notice the man at the window? I didn't catch him at all on the news reel's first running."

"Possibly you're more partial to parades than I am; it bored me so I fell to admiring the architecture of the buildings in the background and was looking directly at the window behind that little stone balcony when its solitary occupant threw out his hands and disappeared with such startling suddenness."

"Humph, too bad your eyes didn't stay where they belonged," Fisk muttered aggrievedly. "Here I'm off duty and you not only make me sit through a second running of half the program but now insist on dragging me off to satisfy your infernal curiosity by a look at the window itself."

"Hard lines." Traherne only grinned at him with a cheerful lack of sympathy. "But that half glimpsed tableau at the window rouses fascinating suppositions."

"Such as?"

"I'll confide some of them after we know whether they've any solid foundations—I'd hate being forced into the position of saying, 'I told you so.'"

"It's a moral certainty we'll find nothing wrong. Besides it's Sunday and there'll be nobody about the building but a possible watchman."

"Have I said I intended going inside? Only mentioned a desire to read the name on the window."

"Yes, but once you've done that you won't be satisfied till you've nosed about inside," Fisk predicted. "I haven't forgotten that you told me your new play was finished and you needed distraction."

Sydney Traherne only laughed, and once the Stanwix Bank and Trust Building was reached proceeded to justify his friend's prediction by first driving slowly past it, while they both easily enough deciphered the gold-lettered legend on the third window, then drawing in to the curb and shutting off his engine.

"Peter Cardigan, Stocks and Bonds," he mused half aloud. "Name mean anything to you?"

"Not an earthly thing," Fisk retorted. "Though I'm becoming increasingly aware that we lunched too lightly—I'm slowly starving."

"So?" Traherne unfeelingly ignored the statement and slipping from the driver's seat, crossed to the Stanwix Building's big closed doors. The inspector watched him for a second, then grumblingly followed.

There was a small bell marked "Watchman" inconspicuously set in the door's ornamental scrollwork, and despite the inspector's protests Traherne pressed it, then, when nothing happened, laid a firmly insistent finger on the bell and left it there. A couple of minutes later his persistence was rewarded by the opening of one leaf of the huge bronze door and the appearance of a heavy shouldered, thick-necked individual, evidently the watchman.

"Sorry to disturb you," Traherne began before the man had time to speak, "but we've an appointment with one of your tenants and the doors seem to be locked."

"They always are, of a Sunday, sir." The watchman stood aside to let them enter, then closed and relocked the open leaf. "There's a small side entrance the tenants mostly use when they've business here after closing hours but being strangers, of course you couldn't know that. Who was it you wanted to see?"

"Mr. Peter Cardigan."

The man scratched a reflective ear. "I don't remember to have seen him come in today. Are you sure the appointment was for his office, sir, and not his apartment?"

"Quite sure," Traherne firmly insisted. "He specifically mentioned the Stanwix building."

"But that could cover the apartment just as well."

"How so?"

"Why, you see, sir, the four top floors are laid out as apartments instead of offices, with Mr. Stanwix's penthouse bungalow a-top the lot."

"And Peter Cardigan lives in one of these apartments?"

"Yes. A big one, I've heard, up on the 22nd floor."

Traherne appeared to silently digest the information before suggesting: "Suppose you 'phone up and ask if Mr. Cardigan is expecting us? Not knowing that his office and home were under the same roof, it's just possible we made a mistake as to what he said."

The request seemed ordinary enough and the man had no cause to doubt the reason given for their visit. He led them back through the emptily echoing hall to a small telephone booth set at a jog of the marble stairs.

"If you'll wait a minute I'll put through a call for Mr. Stanwix' apartment."

"Nice mess we'll be in when the honorable Peter disowns us root and branch," Inspector Fisk muttered, sotto voce, his gaze resting gloomily on the watchman inside the now closed telephone booth.

"I don't imagine that's what's scheduled to happen," Traherne answered. "There was one detail about that window-scene in the news reel that you appeared to miss."

"What was it?"

"Tell you later. The watchman's hanging up."

The man rejoined them, looking decidedly puzzled. "I had young Kent Cardigan on the 'phone and he says his father's away for the week-end. Are you sure the appointment was for today, sir?"

For a second Sydney Traherne's oddly striped eyes studied the man's face, then, apparently satisfied of his intelligence, or discretion, he turned to address Inspector Fisk.

"Better tell him the truth, I think?" It was more than half a question, and the other answered by an assenting nod. "The story of an appointment was pure fiction," Traherne rapidly explained to the puzzled, slightly indignant watchman. "The truth is we're from police headquarters; my friend's Inspector Conway Fisk of the Homicide Bureau, and we've reason to think something may have happened to Peter Cardigan. Can you remember when you saw him last?"

"Why—" The man was plainly suspicious of their abrupt change of character. "Why—if that's true you won't mind showing me your badges or some papers. One has to be careful of strangers, these days."

Satisfied by Inspector Fisk's professional card and a half dozen letters, the watchman's manner lost its wariness and he declared himself willing to answer any questions they chose to put.

"First, were you on duty yesterday afternoon when the parade went by?" Traherne wanted to know.

"Yes. So many offices close early Saturday that half the regular force knocks off at noon and I'm always here from then till the night watchman relieves me at twelve."

"The parade passed at three o'clock," Traherne stated. "Can you remember seeing Mr. Cardigan after that?"

"No, I can't," the watchman decided after a moment's careful thought. "But that doesn't say he didn't go in or out. I wasn't on the ground floor much, as I remember."

"Is there a way of getting to these upper apartments from the office floors of the building, without going out into the street?"

"Yes. That elevator marked 'Private' takes you up to the apartment floors." He indicated the elevator at the extreme left of the long row of doors. "It's used a good deal, but the real apartment entrance is round on the side street."

"Happen to know which method Peter Cardigan favors?"

"Most times I've seen him go out to the street. Week nights I'm only here from six to twelve, so I'm not as well up about the tenants as, say the day doorman, but I do know Mr. Cardigan better than most for he's a habit of coming back after dinner and working nights."

"Not last night?"

"I'm pretty sure not. Fact is, I can't remember seeing Mr. Cardigan all yesterday, though I did see young Mr. Kent going out; he's the son, you know."

"Was he alone?"

"Yes. He didn't use an elevator but walked down, and I ran into him on the stairs."

"What time was this?"

"Hard to say exactly—but it was after the parade went by."

"It was this parade that gave us a hint of something wrong," Traherne hesitated a split-second, then plunged into a brief account of what the news reel had shown, ending with a question: "Can you describe Peter Cardigan?"

"He's a tall, real thin, gray-haired old gentleman— mostly wears dark colored clothes and a little bow tie."

"Sounds like the man at the window. What do you say, inspector? Shall we open the office door and have a look inside?"

"You're bossing this show, and I suppose there's no hope of dinner till your curiosity's satisfied, so we might as well get it over with." Then, to the watchman: "Have you a key to Mr. Cardigan's office door?"

"No, I've only general passkeys, nothing to fit the tenants' private locks; but the cleaning women have to have

'em and when they're off duty they're left in the superintendent's care. If you like to wait here I'll see what he
thinks about opening Mr. Cardigan's door."

"The superintendent lives here on the premises?"

"He's a set of rooms in the basement."

While the watchman was gone Inspector Fisk insisted
on being told of whatever detail in the little scene at the
window Traherne had caught and he himself missed.

"Nothing very definite, only a peculiar blur just above
the man's head an instant before he vanished—it may have
been no more than static, or a flaw in the film."

"But you think it was something else?"

"Possibly."

"Hum-m, Hanged if I see what."

Here the watchman returned accompanied by the building's superintendent and the situation had to be again
explained and Inspector Fisk's credentials shown. Even
then he seemed doubtful about opening Peter Cardigan's
door but finally consented; the watchman running all four
men up in one of the vacant elevators.

At first glance the outer office of the Stock and Bond
firm appeared in perfect order, its three desks stripped and
closed for over the week end, its waste baskets carefully
emptied, all the furniture in its proper place. It was only
when Traherne's questing eye lit on the big safe sunk in a
side wall that he was sure of something amiss; its door was
not quite shut.

He called the superintendent's attention, warning him
against effacing possible finger prints as the man strode
across to pull the heavy door wide open. Inside was such
a dire confusion of tumbled papers and ransacked inner
drawers as to leave no doubt that the safe's contents had
been hastily overturned by someone in too great a hurry
to attempt restitution of anything like order, and at sight
of the safe's wildly tumbled contents Inspector Fisk was

suddenly transformed from a slightly bored on-looker to an alert, experienced police official faced with a possibly criminal problem.

"Open the inner door, superintendent—the safe can wait till later." His suddenly authoritative tone brought instant obedience, the building superintendent hastily fitted a key into the lock under the neatly lettered 'Private' and threw the door wide open so that they could all see into the handsomely furnished inner office.

It was a fairly large room, its two windows, outside one of which could be seen the ornamental balcony rail of the news reel, facing west so that the last rays of the departing sun flooded the place, pitilessly bathing the room's silent occupant with a mellow golden light that horribly accentuated his hideously contorted face and lolling tongue, while his starting eyes appeared to glare an indignant protest against their invasion.

"Strangled!" Inspector Fisk was across the room and kneeling beside the dead man almost before the watchman and superintendent grasped the fact that murder had stalked into their peaceful Sabbath quiet. "Is it Peter Cardigan?"

"Y-es—sir—yes, that's him!" It was the watchman who first recovered the use of his tongue; adding with a touch of bizarre bewilderment: "But he's dead! Choked!"

"With a particularly slender silk cord." Sydney Traherne indicated the lax length of it that appeared to sprout from the dead man's throat, to trail limply across the carpet. "I feared it was the whirl of a slip-noose settling over his head that caused that blur in the film."

The noose itself was so sunk into the dead man's neck that only his blackened face and the loosely trailing end revealed its fatal presence.

"Better leave it in place until the medical examiner comes," Inspector Fisk decided. "Though later on I'll want a sight of the knot used—sometimes they're individual enough in pattern, to help determine who tied them." He rose slowly to his feet, keen blue eyes scanning room, windows, the exact position of the body. "No sign of a struggle—-apparently Mr. Cardigan had no chance to put up a fight."

"No," Traherne's tone was thoughtful. "In that brief glimpse we had of him at the window did he give you the impression of being alone?"

"I believe so. Certainly no one else showed on the screen and if I remember rightly Mr. Cardigan neither spoke, nor turned his head as if there was anyone with him. Three o'clock Saturday afternoon and this is Sunday—queer his family haven't missed him and made inquiries before."

"If you'll remember, sir, young Mr. Kent just now told me his father was away for over the weekend," the watchman here ventured to remind him.

"That's true, and by the same token I think we ought to go straight to the Cardigan apartment—we need to ask this son of the family a few questions. Can you take charge here, superintendent, and see that nothing's disturbed until the medical examiner and men from headquarters arrive?"

"Surely."

"Then I'll 'phone at once." He turned to Sydney Traherne; "Or do you want a quiet hour alone here, first?"

The playwright's brindled black and silver head shook a slightly hesitant negative.

"No, I agree with you about an immediate visit to Peter Cardigan's apartment."

2

DAPHNE

"Murdered? Oh, no, indeed you must be mistaken! Nobody could possibly want to murder an inoffensive man like my brother."

"Perhaps you think he tied a cord round his own neck?" the inspector sarcastically inquired.

"No," Miss Camellia Cardigan's tone was sweetly reasonable, as the faded blue eyes set in a long pale face regarded them almost pityingly. "No. It must have been an accident. *That* could happen even to a Cardigan, but we never commit suicide or allow ourselves to be murdered—*never*. We're a very conservative family."

"Well, violent death's hardly a thing any family cultivates as a general habit—there has to be a first time," Fisk dryly pointed out. "Now, perhaps you'll be good enough to tell us when you last saw Mr. Peter Cardigan—and anything you can about his plans for yesterday."

Instead of answering either question Camellia Cardigan quite suddenly gave free rein to the grief or shock temporarily held at bay by her indignant repudiation of his suggestion of murder.

"Peter dead! I simply can't believe it!" she sobbed, mopping streaming eyes with a particularly scratchy looking handkerchief. "Where's Kent? Why isn't he here to uphold me in the hour of sorrow?"

"That's the first humanly sensible word she's uttered! Where *is* Kent Cardigan? You'll remember the watchman told us he left his father's office after the parade went by yesterday afternoon."

"Not quite that," Traherne instantly corrected. "He only mentioned seeing Peter Cardigan's son leave the building, not the office itself."

"Practically the same thing." The inspector cast a hopelessly discouraged eye over the weeping Camellia, then crossed to the door through which they had entered and opening it, disappeared in search of the maid servant who had admitted them. He had not far to look, the girl was hovering suspiciously close to the drawing room door and made not the slightest attempt to hide the fact that she had been eavesdropping.

"Oh, sir, isn't it awful to think of poor Mr. Cardigan lying dead like that in his office? Whoever could have killed him, do you think?"

"Too early to hazard an answer to that question." The inspector was studying her pretty, rather intelligent little face. "Was he a popular man, one who had many friends?"

"Well, not what you'd call many friends, sir," she appeared to weigh the matter before adding:

"Mr. Cardigan wasn't one for much entertaining of company—most of the folks who visited him came on business, just slipping in and out quiet like. But he was a nice man to work for, very nice."

"You've been in the household some time?"

"Yes, sir, nearly two years."

"And the family—how many are there?"

"Only the three, sir. Mr. Cardigan, Miss Camellia, and young Mr. Kent."

"The son." Fisk nodded. "Where is he, by the way?"

"Upstairs in the Stanwix penthouse, sir, he went up about half an hour ago."

"The two families are friendly, then?"

"Oh, very! Mr. Kent went to school and to college with Myron Stanwix—they're nearly like brothers, all three of 'em."

"Three?"

"Counting Mr. Stanger, sir, the young man Miss Faith Stanwix is going to marry."

"Here, let me get this straight," Inspector Fisk growled. "There were only three members of the Cardigan family— Peter Cardigan himself, his unmarried sister, and his son Kent?" Then, as the girl's head bobbed assentingly: "And the Stanwix's who own this building and live in a pent-house bungalow on the top of it are intimate friends. How many in that family?"

"The same number as here, sir, only with them it's the father and a son and daughter. You see, sir"—with the air of one imparting valuable information, "Mr. Stanwix and Mr. Cardigan married two ladies who were ever such close friends, more like sisters so I've heard, and it was through them that the two men got to be such close friends."

"Both the wives dead now?"

"Yes, sir, quite a few years ago."

"Well, the family history doesn't appear to enter into the case, still one never knows. Don't telephone the news of his father's death to Kent Cardigan; we'll go up present-ly and tell him ourselves." He refrained from mentioning his desire to catch Kent's first reaction to the news. "But first I'd like you to answer a few questions. You spoke of visitors who came here very quietly—did you mean that only Peter Cardigan saw them, not his sister or son?"

"Never the ones who came on business," the girl ex-plained. "Of course Miss Camellia and Mr. Kent both have their own friends and sometimes people came especially to play cards with Mr. Cardigan himself—but the ones I meant were different. They'd just send in their cards to

Mr. Cardigan and if he wasn't busy, see him for twenty minutes or so—they never stopped long and they never went to any room but his study."

"Humph!" Conway Fisk seemed to consider the information important enough to deserve careful digestion. "Can you describe these visitors, their general class or type, I mean?"

"Only that they were mostly quietly dressed—though not quite always—and that—well, it's a queer thing to say, but sometimes I had a feeling they didn't like being looked at too close."

"All men?"

"No, sir, a good few were ladies."

"Do you know if any of these, shall we say 'quiet' visitors, ever quarreled with Peter Cardigan?"

"Not that I know of, sir."

"Humph—and there's been no recent family quarrel?"

"No indeed, sir, they weren't a family that ever quarreled."

"No trouble between Kent Cardigan and his father?"

"Oh, dear no!" the little maid sounded positively shocked by the suggestion. "There was never a cross word between the two of them."

"Sounds quite a model family," Fisk commented. "Now, how does one reach the Stanwix home from here?"

"Taking the elevator's the best way, though of course there're stairs; they only take you up to the roof, not inside the house like the elevator does.

After a few more questions and a last futile attempt to extract something helpful from the weeping Camellia, Fisk and Sydney Traherne went up by the elevator to which the solicitous little maid directed them—to be received in the outer hall of the Stanwix home by a tall, impressively correct butler.

"Mr. Kent Cardigan is calling here, I believe?" Inspector Fisk asked.

For a second the man hesitated, perhaps unable to quite gage their social standing, then answered evasively:

"If you'll wait one moment, sir, I'll inquire."

"No." Fisk checked his silent progress toward the main portion of the big, sprawling bungalow. "We're from headquarters," he favored the butler with a fleeting glimpse of his police badge. "Don't announce us. Simply point out the room where Kent Cardigan is and say nothing to anyone else."

"It's most irregular," the man objected.

"Police matters frequently are," Fisk retorted. "Kindly do as I say."

"The young gentlemen are in the library, sir. If you'll come this way."

He led them through a wide hall that spread half across the southern face of the house and was evidently used as a general lounging place, its many low tables, groups of big chairs, and profusion of freshly cut flowers lending it an air of used and intimate comfort. Diagonally across from the door by which they entered was another closed one, before which the butler paused, disapproval plainly evinced in look and bearing. With a muttered, "Irregular, most irregular!" he threw the door wide, standing aside to let them enter and reclosing it behind them.

The library's only occupant was a dark, sleek-haired man somewhere in his late twenties, who stood near one of the long French windows idly fingering a book. At the sound made by the closing door he turned, showing a cleanly chiseled, olive-skinned face that expressed surprise and a touch of annoyance, at the abrupt entry of two complete strangers.

"Yes?" the tone held an arrogant question.

"Are you Kent Cardigan?"

"I am not." He came toward them, the book still held in long restless fingers that nervously flicked at its leaves. "If it interests you to know, I'm Myron Stanwix—and very much at a loss to account for your unannounced presence here. What do you want?"

"We have business, of grave importance, with Kent Cardigan," Fisk's pleasantly casual voice had taken on a sudden crisp authority. "Where is he?"

"On the terrace—no, here."

As he spoke two men of about his own age came in through the open French window. One was tall, largely built without being in the least heavy, a superb blond Viking of a man; the other shorter, much more slender, with indeterminate drab colored hair and cool gray eyes under whimsically pointed eyebrows.

"Someone to see you, Kent," Myron Stanwix addressed the tall young Viking who had paused just inside the window.

"To see me?" he echoed uncomprehendingly.

"We're the bearers of bad news—which you'd perhaps rather hear in private."

"No. These are my friends, I've no secrets from them." Kent Cardigan's bright blue gaze flashed from one to the other of the two strangers confronting him, dwelt a second on Sydney Traherne's quietly noncommittal face, then settled on Inspector Fisk. "What news can you possibly have for me?"

"The fact that your father is lying in his office—murdered!"

There was a soft little crash as the book fell from Myron Stanwix's suddenly relaxed fingers, but Kent Cardigan himself took the news without a visible tremor—only his wide shoulders went back as if resistant to an unforeseen blow. There was a moment of tense silence, broken by Kent's defiant denial:

"I don't believe you! My father is not in town!"

"No? May I ask how you gained that impression?"

"He telephoned yesterday afternoon to say he'd been unexpectedly called out of town and meant staying away over the week-end."

"Who took the message?"

"I did."

"Answering the phone yourself?"

"Yes."

"So that no one else spoke to your father?"

"No one."

"Aren't your servants in the habit of answering the telephone?"

"Naturally, but I happened to be in the hall when it rang."

"At what time was this?"

"Somewhere around five, I think."

"Did Mr. Cardigan say where he was at the time?"

"No."

"Or with whom?"

"No."

"Simply left town for a couple of days without so much as a toothbrush?" The inspector's voice was frankly skeptical.

"My father always kept a packed bag in his office," young Cardigan resentfully explained. "It was nothing unusual for him to be called away at a moment's notice."

"Humph! And you're ready to swear it was his voice on the wire?"

"See here, I'm not in the habit of having my word questioned. I suppose you're police officers, but that fact doesn't entitle you to imply that I'm lying about my father's 'phone message."

"Perhaps not, yet it's a bit difficult to see how a man who'd been dead for two hours could telephone you at five o'clock to say he meant leaving town."

"How do you know he died before five o'clock? That is, if he's actually dead."

Instead of answering Fisk suddenly switched to another line of inquiry. "Had Peter Cardigan any enemies—had he recently received any threatening letters?"

"Certainly not! Dad's business was a perfectly respectable stock and bond concern—that had nothing in common with a bucket-shop! His clients have always been wealthy, conservative people who, under his advice invested in legitimate securities without taking any wild flings in the Stock Market."

"Meaning, they weren't apt to get ruined and in consequence hold a grudge against Peter Cardigan as the man responsible?"

"I tell you there wasn't a particle of hanky-panky about the firm!"

"You're speaking as a member?" Conway Fisk was remembering those unobtrusive business visitors of whom the Cardigan maid had told him; they hardly sounded like the conservative investors described by Kent Cardigan.

"No, father wanted me to get experience elsewhere before joining his firm."

"Your father's outer office has three desks," Fisk stated. "Who occupies them?"

"A stenographer and two outside bond salesmen."

"Really? Then the firm's business doesn't consist wholly of advising wealthy clients? It occasionally goes after new blood? Now." He paused a second, quietly intent eyes on Kent Cardigan's face. "When did you last see your father?"

"Yesterday morning at breakfast. Murray Sanger," a jerk of his big blond head indicated the cool-eyed man of pleasantly irregular features, "intended looking at a new car he meant buying, so he stopped in for breakfast and dad shared the meal."

"You later on inspected the car?"

"Yes."

"And during the afternoon went to your father's office."

"I did, though I don't see how you knew it."

"At what time?" Fisk quietly ignored the point.

"Nearly four, I should think."

"See anyone?"

"No. The office door was locked and though I knocked repeatedly no one answered. As it was Saturday I decided the whole office force had gone home."

Here Murray Sanger, who a moment before had consulted his watch, for the first time volunteered a remark.

"Don't you think we should go into some other room, Kent? Or else lock the door? Faith's about due and we don't want her barging in and getting the news without preparation."

"Faith?" Inspector Fisk caught at the name, then turned to Myron Stanwix. "She's your sister?"

"Yes. She's been away on a week's visit and wrote she'd be home in time for dinner tonight." His tone had completely lost its first arrogance, and now betrayed a touch of anxiety. "Peter Cardigan has always been almost like an uncle to us—we don't want Faith hearing of his—death, too suddenly."

"Why not tell the butler—" Fisk was interrupted by the abrupt opening of the hall door; its polished dark wood framing a slender, scarlet-clad girl who stood poised for a second, big brown eyes fleeing wildly from one to another of the grouped men, then, lighting on Murray Sanger they lost their look of strained terror and she covered the intervening space, with the soft rush of a homing bird.

"What's wrong?" she demanded, from the safe shelter of his welcoming arm. "Not—not daddy?"

"No. Uncle Peter," it was her brother who answered. "How did you know anything had happened?"

"Fargo. He looked pale as a ghost and tried to keep me from coming in here. Where's daddy?"

"Not home from the Country Club yet. He hasn't heard."

"Oh!" With a conscience-stricken little gasp Faith suddenly freed herself. "I brought a guest back with me, she's in the hall and must think I've gone crazy—but Fargo's manner frightened me. I thought something had happened to you." A shy smile brushed the soft red lips as her adoring gaze dwelt on Murray Sanger, and was reluctantly dragged away by the necessity of playing hostess. "Do please bring her in, Myron."

The slender dark brother who looked so much like Faith herself went into the hall, returning with a woman whose beauty was like a flame lighting the big dusky room where twilight shadows had begun to gather. Rather tall, with superbly flowing lines of rounded breast and supple, slenderly turned hips, she seemed of another race or generation than the modern boyishly athletic type. Yet the creamy throat, like smooth new ivory, and the face with its great brilliant eyes and delicately perfect features was unmistakably young. While waiting she had, for some feminine reason not difficult to guess, removed her hat and it was the blazing, coppery glory of her hair that lent her beauty such an arresting, flame-like quality.

"Daphne dear, forgive my deserting you like that." Faith went to her, affectionately linking arms with her guest and turning to face the slightly awestruck group of men. "This is Daphne Fane, my very newest and dearest friend."

3

THE STANWIX BUTLER

"Now you've got me into this case, do you intend seeing me through?" Conway Fisk played rather uninterestedly with his steak as he eyed Traherne across the table.

After leaving the Stanwix penthouse they had paid a second and much longer visit to Peter Cardigan's office, where medical examiner, police photographer, and finger print expert had in the meantime been extremely busy. Then, urged by the inspector's insistent demand for food, the two friends had retired to the corner table of a favorite chop-house; where Fisk's appetite appeared to have quite suddenly deserted him. Traherne glanced up from the mixed grill to the excellency of which he was doing slow but full justice.

"Didn't I tell you this afternoon I'd just finished a new play? I'm badly in need of something to take my mind off, exit R.—cross L. to chair upstage—excited voices off stage L.—and all the rest of the distracting mechanics of an otherwise enthralling profession. Of course I'll see you through to the finish."

"Right." The assurance instantly restored Fisk's languishing appetite; he bestowed a new and thorough attention on the plate before him, presently remarking between bites: "Odd, your being the first to catch that murder was being done in the very eye of the camera, so to speak. It's

a wonder somebody didn't catch it in the projecting room
or when the news reel was cut."

"Why? Naturally they were watching the important
thing, the parade; the little scene at an upper window was
too inconspicuous to catch any but a bored and roving
eye."

"Queer time the murderer picked—when his victim was
standing in full view of anyone happening to look up from
the street."

"He, or she, doubtless reasoned that the parade would
absorb everybody's attention and Peter Cardigan's position, with his back squarely turned, was too good an opportunity to miss."

"Must have been premeditated; otherwise the cord
wouldn't have been so immediately available."

"Unless it belonged in the office, which seems unlikely.
Did you notice the peculiar knot used? One very similar to
those of the Hindu Kali's Thugee worshipers."

"I noticed it was peculiar. It must have required a pretty strong hand, by the way, to jerk Peter Cardigan back
like that and throttle him without attracting the attention
of anyone in a neighboring office."

"Not necessarily. He was completely off guard and any
sounds of a scuffle would be more or less drowned by the
noise from the street. Besides we don't yet know if either
of the adjacent offices were occupied at that particular
hour." Traherne pushed aside his almost emptied plate. "I
wish we could be certain whether or not Peter Cardigan
thought himself alone."

"You mean, if there was someone actually in the office
with him it must have been a friend, a person he had no
reason to fear?"

"Isn't that fact self evident?"

"Admitted. And if we were sure of the point it would
considerably narrow our inquiry—but as it is we've got to

remember that the murderer may have been a total stranger, say a sneak thief who entered the office, saw the old man standing at the window and killed him, so as to leave a free field for rifling the safe."

"Faulty reasoning," Traherne reproved him. "First, sneak thieves don't kill unless they're cornered and Cardigan didn't turn his head before he was jerked back—therefore he didn't see his assailant creeping up behind him, and second, as you yourself pointed out a moment ago, silk cords strong enough to strangle a man aren't things one commonly totes about in one's pocket. No, Fisk, the crime wasn't a mere chance affair; somebody deliberately planned to kill. The only point that's doubtful is, whether Peter Cardigan knew of the murderer's presence in the room, or whether he stole in while the old man stood watching the parade."

"It's a pity we haven't been able to get hold of the stenographer and outside salesmen—they ought to know how much money was in the safe and what valuable papers, if any, are missing; the thief seems to have made a pretty clean sweep, there weren't many stocks or bonds left lying round."

"The office files were also a bit ill nourished, and there wasn't any sign of a heavy correspondence such as you'd expect to find in a business of that nature." He paused, to veto their waiter's suggestion of a dessert and ordered coffee instead. "Strike you as singular that while all the trash baskets had been emptied, your man found a crumpled envelope addressed to Kent Cardigan in one of them?"

"To tell the truth I didn't pay it much attention. Why?"

"Well—" Traherne meditatively sugared his coffee, then lighted a cigarette. "It hadn't been through the mail and was addressed in Peter Cardigan's own hand writing—as I learned by comparing it with samples your man supplied from the desk—now why should the old gentleman write to the son he was seeing daily? Why not convey whatever message he had to give by word of mouth?"

"Hum-m—the point hadn't occurred to me," Fisk admitted. "And what became of the letter belonging in the envelope? Assuming, of course, that it originally contained a letter and not a sum of money or a receipt of some kind. Young Cardigan denied being in his father's office yesterday—yet the envelope addressed to him must have been dropped in the trash basket after they were emptied yesterday morning."

"Quite so. And if Kent Cardigan's telling the truth it seems the murderer was the one who dropped it. Now why such interest in the Cardigan family correspondence?"

"You're working toward a theory of the crime covering something besides plain robbery," the inspector's tone was slightly aggrieved; he had been hoping for an uninvolved case of theft. "Why not wait until we've seen Mark Stanwix before you start hunting complications? He was the dead man's closest friend and ought to be able to post us on business and personal matters. Wonder where he is, by the bye? Queer that he's neither gone home nor sent any word."

"Why? He's no legitimate reason for supposing he's needed."

"No, of course not. I'll 'phone again presently and see if he's turned up yet. Likely to prove an interesting type if he's anything like his son and daughter; they struck me as a likeable pair."

"Especially the girl."

Fisk nodded. "Seems a sweet little thing. I wonder why she picked Murray Sanger with the much more spectacular Kent Cardigan in the offing—if she had a choice, that is." Then, after a few minutes' absorption in the proper lighting of a first after-dinner cigar: "What'd you think of the flame-haired lady?"

"You used the word that best describes her—spectacular. What a pair she and Kent Cardigan would make!"

"Oh, there can't be two opinions as to her beauty," the inspector conceded. "I was referring more to her character, social position and background, she struck me as a trifle hard to place."

"So? Still, as she's a complete stranger to all but Faith Stanwix she scarcely enters in, does she? At the moment there are a couple of other people who interest me more than the flame-haired lady."

"For instance?"

"Well—" Traherne slowly poured himself a second cup of coffee. "Just in passing, I wonder why Myron Stanwix was sufficiently startled by news of Mr. Cardigan's death to drop a book he was holding."

"Suddenly hearing that an old friend's been murdered is enough to startle anyone."

"Yet Kent Cardigan never turned a hair. If he felt any natural grief he certainly succeeded in hiding it."

"You're not suspecting him of a hand in his father's death, are you?"

"Merely curious. The person I'm most concerned about is the Stanwix butler. How'd he know there was anything seriously wrong?"

"What makes you think he did?"

"When little Faith Stanwix dashed in she declared the butler's attitude had frightened her—now if you think back you'll remember that in asking for Kent Cardigan we said nothing about any trouble, and during our talk in the library we were too far away from the hall door, which was tightly closed, for him to have overheard what was said— then why did he try to keep Faith Stanwix from entering?"

"Don't forget I'd told him we were from headquarters. He probably thought young Cardigan had got into trouble with the police."

"Even so, he wasn't Faith's brother or sweetheart. An outsider's trouble with the police ought not to disorganize a trained servant. I tell you there's something fishy about the man. Did you look at him at all?"

"No," Fisk admitted after a little reflection. "Who ever does look at a butler? I couldn't so much as tell you if the man's yellow, or white, simply gained an impression of the last word in swank butlers."

"Oh, there was nothing off color about the man's get up, but he'd the physique of a trained athlete, and the face of a matinee idol—ever know a respectable butler who boasted such a combination?

"You're drawing on that playwright's imagination of yours," Inspector Fisk accused. "Though I'll humor you by taking a closer look at the fellow next time we visit the Stanwix bungalow."

4

The Letter

When Inspector Fisk next 'phoned the owner had returned and was anxiously awaiting an interview.

Mark Stanwix strongly resembled his son and daughter, except that he was of a more rugged, virile type; his dark hair shaggy and, aggressively alive, his fine eyes possessed of a piercing quality that lacked any softness or subtlety. They hinted at an understrain of hardness, perhaps cruelty; an effect in no wise contradicted by his high-arched, delicately-nostriled nose and wide thin mouth.

With him, when Sydney Traherne and Inspector Fisk were admitted, was a small, foppishly slender little man, dressed with the accurate perfection of a fashion plate; Whitney Page, a lawyer whose very delicacy of appearance often deceived his opponents into underestimating his powers, both defensive and offensive.

"I included Mr. Page in our conference because he was Peter Cardigan's personal lawyer as well as my own," Mark Stanwix explained when the preliminary introductions were over. "Also he is, so far as I know, the only living person besides myself, acquainted with the contents of Cardigan's somewhat singular will."

"You think this document may in some way affect our investigation of Peter Cardigan's murder?" Inspector Fisk accepted his host's offer of a cigar and settled into one of

31

the leather chairs of Mark Stanwix' study; a room on the opposite side of the bungalow from the library which they had seen earlier in the evening.

"I should hardly care to commit myself to an opinion on that point," Mark Stanwix cautiously hedged. "Still, under the circumstances I thought you ought to hear a certain clause of the will." He turned to the restlessly fidgeting lawyer. "Mind giving them the necessary data, Page?"

"Not at all." Instead of taking a chair Whitney Page perched on the edge of a table, twirling a gold-rimmed monocle between white, exquisitely manicured fingers as he commenced. "Please understand that the will in question was made some years ago—when Kent Cardigan was only nineteen to be exact—and leaves the entire estate to him, with one proviso. Kent is to enjoy only the interest until he reaches the age of twenty-five, at which time he is to be handed the key to a certain safety deposit box registered in his father's name—and, after his examination of the contents of said box, Kent is to enter into unrestricted possession of the estate, free and clear except for certain bequests to old servants and a generous allowance paid to Miss Camellia Cardigan during her lifetime.

"This clause touching the key is still effective? Kent Cardigan hasn't reached the designated age?"

"No. His twenty-fifth birthday falls on Wednesday of this coming week."

"I'd have guessed him older."

"Probably because of his size. As a matter of fact Kent's the youngest of the three 'Inseparables' as he, Myron Stanwix, and Murray Sanger have been nicknamed since their earliest schooldays."

"Does Kent Cardigan know the contents of his father's will?"

"Not unless Peter Cardigan enlightened him—a thing he expressly warned *me* against ever considering."

"Hm-m and may I ask if either of you gentlemen have the slightest inkling what this special safety deposit box contains?"

"Speaking personally, I haven't the vaguest idea."

"Nor I," Mark Stanwix seconded the lawyer's denial.

Whereupon Inspector Fisk retired into a meditative little silence, the others watching him. Whitney Page with an ill-concealed impatience that tightened all his small, bland features, betrayed an underlying sharpness of bone structure that materially changed the aspect of his entire face.

"Considering Peter Cardigan's unexplained murder, perhaps you'd hardly feel it a breach of trust to forestall Kent's birthday and give him the deposit key at once?" The Inspector's tone was more hopeful than expectant.

"Not possible," Mark Stanwix flashed back without a second's hesitation. "As his closest friend, Peter told me it was vitally important that Kent should not have access to that particular box until he was twenty-five."

"When did he make that statement?"

"Two, perhaps three years ago."

"Possibly it was meant to cover a matter of a couple of years, not days."

"Nevertheless I insist on his wishes being respected, not only as regards the safety deposit box but also touching his cremation and the disposal of his ashes."

"You're referring to some other clause in the will?"

"Yes. One that expressly enjoins his executors—Whitney Page and myself—to see that his body is cremated as speedily as the law allows and the ashes, enclosed in a certain urn, bestowed in his family vault in the Sleepy Hollow Cemetery at Tarrytown."

"The autopsy and inquest formalities may slightly delay the execution of that clause," Inspector Fisk declared. "As to the other—the opening of the deposit box—I hardly see how it bears on our investigation, though I admit I'd like knowing what's inside that box without waiting until Wednesday."

"Quite impossible!" There was a decisive snap in Mark Stanwix' tone. "Peter's wishes must be strictly observed."

Fisk let the point drop for the moment, not considering it vital enough to force an issue.

"There's another little matter that we've so far neglected—purely in the way of routine work we must ascertain the exact whereabouts of everyone connected with Peter Cardigan, at the precise time of his death."

"Surely you're not suspecting any of us?" Mark Stanwix' fine eyes flashed resentfully.

"Why should I? In this particular instance the collecting of alibis is a simply formal matter, but one which can't be neglected. Now, Mr. Stanwix, if you'll kindly start the ball rolling by stating where you were at three o'clock yesterday afternoon?"

"Three o'clock? Why such emphasis on that exact time? I've always understood that after the lapse of more than twenty-four hours, even a doctor can't be certain of the precise hour at which a person died."

"We've other data than the medical examiner's opinion," the inspector assured him, without going into particulars. "Mind answering my question as to your whereabouts?"

"It so happens that I can tell you within a block or two. I was in a taxi on my way to the Grand Central to catch the 3:10 for Irvington."

"And you caught it?"

"I seldom miss trains," Stanwix informed him with just a breath of the arrogance they had earlier noted in his son. "I caught the 3:10 with a comfortable margin—walked from the Irvington station to my Country Club because I felt in need of exercise, and later on played a round of golf and dined there."

"You make it a habit to use the trains rather than driving out to this Country Club?"

"No. As a matter of fact I generally drive but at the moment my own car's under repairs. That's why I took the train both times—yesterday and today."

"You, yesterday, rode out with some acquaintance, perhaps?"

"On the contrary I saw no one I knew."

"H-um! Pity there's no one to verify your whereabouts at three on Saturday. Still it hardly appears to matter. And you, Mr. Page?"

"I was at a picture show; for which fact I must ask you to accept my unsupported word as I was also, quite alone."

"Then, unless there's some further information you can give me regarding Peter Cardigan or his will, we'll next question the young people about yesterday afternoon."

"As you like. They're all in the library, I think."

Before he and Sydney Traherne had quite reached the hall door, Inspector Fisk turned to put a last question.

"Do you know if Peter Cardigan recently quarreled with anyone, or if he had made any recent enemies?"

"Not so far as I know."

The answer seemed to satisfy Fisk and Traherne wondered if he himself was unduly suspicious in fancying a note of hesitancy in Mark Stanwix' voice.

In the library Daphne Fane, Faith Stanwix, her brother and Murray Sanger were playing bridge, and offered not the slightest objection to stopping their game when Inspector Fisk explained what was wanted.

"With the best will in the world, I'm hanged if I know where I was at exactly three o'clock," Myron Stanwix acknowledged after several reflective draws at his cigarette.

"Somewhere on Fifth Avenue, buying, or rather hunting for ties of a certain shade, is the best I can do."

"If you remember which stores you were in some of the salespeople may be able to help us out," Fisk hopefully suggested, then wrote down a short list of the shops young Stanwix remembered visiting. "And you, Mr. Sanger?" He turned to Faith's fiancé, note book in hand.

"I've an almost suspiciously perfect alibi." As Murray Sanger's deepset gray eyes and wide, flexible mouth crinkled into a smile holding a certain Pan-like, almost impish attraction, the inspector for the first time quite understood Faith's undisguised devotion; the man possessed a winning charm far exceeding that of mere regularity of feature. "I was in one of the elevators going down to the apartment entrance and the boy running it—Paddy's the youngster's name, by the way— asked for the exact time because his relief was due at three and Paddy wanted to get away in time to see the parade, the music of which we could already hear."

"You gave it him?"

"Yes. After looking at my watch I told Paddy it was just three o'clock and another passenger checked my timepiece with his own."

"Thereby proving that you couldn't have been elsewhere at that particular hour." Fisk found himself warmly responding to Sanger's engaging smile. "Not that any of this alibi business is more than a mere form—but one that rules and regulations insist on. And now, for the ladies. You were away from New York I think, Miss Stanwix?"

"Officially but not actually," Faith told him. "I've been spending a week with some friends in Greenwich, Connecticut, but on Saturday several of us drove into town for matinées or shopping. I think, though I'm not really sure, that I was in Stern Brothers around three o'clock."

"Do you know which department?"

"Haven't the faintest idea. We'd arranged to meet at the Biltmore at five, so earlier in the afternoon I paid no especial attention to the time."

"And was Miss Fane with the party who drove in?"

"Yes, but I used my own roadster and had left New York for the return trip before the time you're interested in."

"So you were somewhere on the road—alone?"

"Yes to both questions."

"That more or less accounts for all of you but Kent Cardigan. Anyone happen to know where he was?"

"Not after about one o'clock," Murray Sanger volunteered. "As I think he told you, we looked at a car together yesterday morning, decided against buying it, and separated, Kent saying he'd a luncheon engagement and refusing to let me tag along."

"We'll have to find out if he kept it. Where is he now, do you know?"

"With his aunt, I think. He left us immediately after you'd told us of his father's death, saying Miss Camellia would need looking after."

"About the type of alibis one usually encounters in a murder inquiry," Fisk grumbled on their way down to the Cardigan apartment. "Apparently no human being ever notices what they're doing at any specific time."

"Probably you don't yourself," Traherne retorted. "Life would be unbearable if we lived it with one eye always on the clock. Stop grousing and be thankful that at least one member of the group possesses a water tight alibi."

"Meaning Murray Sanger? Well, let's hope Kent Cardigan can furnish one half as good."

As it happened young Cardigan's alibi proved to be almost, if not quite, as perfect as his friend's; he declared himself to have been in Schrafft's Fifty-eighth street store hungrily waiting for a certain lady who had promised to lunch with him.

"She'd agreed to meet me at two o'clock, so by three I was next door to starvation and looking at my watch every second minute," he told them when questioned. "I held out till quarter past three, then gave her up and lunched alone."

"And on the stroke of three?"

"I was reproachfully asking the store's pretty little cashier why her sex were invariably late for an appointment—and pointing out on my watch dial the gruesome fact that I'd been waiting a full hour and was nearing a state of collapse."

"Sounds as if you'd filled in the time with a mild flirtation. The cashier will probably remember and be able to check up your story," Fisk suppressed a slightly sympathetic grin. "Have you succeeded in getting hold of any of your father's office force?"

"Not yet. Beastly habit New Yorkers have of all leaving home on a Sunday."

"Inconvenient, but how else would Coney Island and all the other resorts keep running? Is your aunt well enough to see us?"

Kent went to inquire and presently returned with Miss Camellia, still very damp about the eyes but otherwise much more normal than when they had last seen her.

Questioned about the previous day, she told them that her brother had lunched at home, then, contrary to his usual custom on a Saturday, returned to his office saying that he had an important business appointment which might detain him until nearly dinner time. He had said nothing about leaving town so that she had been slightly surprised when, on her return from a theatre, Kent told her his father had just telephoned to say he would be away until Monday.

"Yet I understand it was a thing he often did," Fisk put in. "Leave town on short notice, I mean."

"Oh, dear yes! He was a perfect slave to business and couldn't ever make any definite plans ahead. If he did business always interfered and prevented his carrying them out. But I've something much more important than that to tell you." Miss Camellia sank limply into a chair and covered her eyes for a moment, then looked up with an apologetic little smile. "I'm afraid I was rude when you first told me about—about what had happened. You see I simply couldn't believe it was as you said; that somebody had deliberately killed my brother."

"Natural, perfectly natural," he assured her, anxious to get on with whatever she had to tell.

"Still, I should have remembered that Peter had a terrible quarrel only a few days ago. The reason I knew about it was because I heard him walking up and down in his room in the very middle of the night and went in to see if he was sick. Before he saw me I heard Peter swearing to himself, I didn't quite catch what he said but it sounded as if he was swearing, and then I heard him say: 'To condemn me like that—to believe I lied—so help me God I'll never forgive him!' Then he saw me and was most disagreeable. He said I'd no business sneaking into his room without knocking, and when I insisted on knowing what was wrong he told me he'd quarreled with someone and couldn't sleep for thinking about it."

"With whom?"

"Peter wouldn't tell me that. He wouldn't even say if it was with anyone I knew. Still, I thought might help you to discover who did—it. And besides, but perhaps I ought not to tell you that." She glanced doubtfully at her nephew who answered the look by crossing to stand close beside her, a large reassuring hand on her trembling shoulder.

"Better tell them anything you can, Aunty, there's no knowing what may help."

"Then—at lunch yesterday Peter opened some mail that had come while he was at the office and there was one letter that upset him terribly. I happened to be looking at him when he opened it because the envelope had a wide black border like a mourning envelope, and I wondered who was dead. Peter tore it open and then, when he'd opened out the sheet it contained, I thought he was going to faint he looked so queer and white, but he didn't, he only drank some water, crumpled the paper up in his hand and left the table."

"Did you catch even a glimpse of the letter?" Fisk anxiously demanded.

"Why—that's what seemed so peculiar, it wasn't really a letter at all. When I jumped up and went to Peter thinking he was going to faint, I couldn't help seeing the black-edged sheet in his hand hadn't any writing on it, but only some kind of a drawing."

"Humph, and at sight of it Peter Cardigan came near fainting," the inspector meditated aloud. "Yes, I'll say peculiar's a mild way of putting it. You say he took the paper away with him when he left the table?"

"Yes."

"H-um—it wasn't found in his office. Perhaps you'll let us take a look in his room, Mr. Cardigan?"

"Of course. Study or bed room?"

"Both, I think, but we'll start with the study."

5

An Enameled Vanity Case

Kent Cardigan stopped short on the threshold of his father's study. The room had obviously been searched by someone in a desperate hurry and scattered papers littered the floor from desk to wide open window.

"So," Sydney Traherne was the first to recover from their surprise. "Our friend the murderer didn't find what he was after in Peter Cardigan's office."

"But how did he get in?" Kent's bewilderment was either perfectly genuine or a magnificent bit of acting. "The front hall has been under our eyes all evening, no stranger could possibly have passed through it without our seeing them, and I happen to be positive that two of the maids have blocked the only other entrance—through the kitchen."

"Remains, the window." Traherne crossed to it and cast a reflective eye over the immaculate sill and window fastenings.

"I suppose it would be possible to let oneself down from the roof by means of a rope—providing one possessed a cool head and the necessary nerve," Inspector Fisk rather doubtfully suggested. "What's the topography of the roof just over this apartment?"

"Part of the Stanwix flower garden," Kent answered, "with plenty of shrubs and small trees to give the necessary cover and shield anyone from the bungalow windows."

41

"It could be done, I imagine," Traherne had been leaning out through the window, looking both up at the roof only a comparatively short distance above their heads, and down at the sidewalk twenty-two floors below. "Happen to own a flashlight?"

"Yes, I'll get it from my room."

While he was gone Traherne grinned sardonically at his puzzled friend.

"What price a sneak-thief and simple robbery-motive now?"

Fisk only glared, scorning a retort and letting Traherne manipulate the torch which Kent brought back in a minute or two. By its light they could see a foot-wide ledge running along the face of the building just beneath the apartment windows.

"That's a possible mode of entry, though it would take the devil's own nerve to negotiate at this height from the ground." Traherne played the torch-ray back and forth along the ledge. "Notice the little cluster of straws in that angle of the stonework? I've an idea that's all that remains of a bird's nest which the thief demolished in passing. And there's another open window less than twenty feet away—happen to know what it opens on?"

Kent Cardigan leaned out to count windows, then announced that the open one in question belonged to the public hallway giving access to one of the building's enclosed circular emergency staircases.

"Then the intruder could easily enough have made use of that particular window without being a resident of the building."

"Yes, I suppose so, and with a little care he'd probably not be seen for there're seldom many people in the halls."

"No use searching this room," Fisk decided. "It's already been thoroughly gone over. I'll send a finger print man up from headquarters tomorrow, but I doubt he'll be able to find anything. How about your father's bed room?"

They half expected to find that room also overhauled and were pleasantly surprised to discover it quite undisturbed. Sending Kent out of the room the inspector examined it with the skilled speed born of long experience, while Sydney Traherne casually perched on a convenient table edge, offering helpful, or sardonic comments but taking no active part in the search. Only one slightly puzzling item rewarded Inspector Fisk's efforts—an expensive looking black and white enameled vanity case.

"Now what the deuce is that doing here?" He extended it on an inquiring palm. "Do you think it's a keepsake of his dead wife?"

"Dead wife my eye—" Traherne scoffed at the sentimental suggestion. "In the first place it's obviously brand new and in the second, they didn't make costly toys of that type when the lady was alive. No, I fear me we've uncovered a dark secret of Peter's past—there's evidently a woman, or more probably a girl, lurking somewhere in the background."

"Now why put the worst possible construction on the thing?" his friend inquired reproachfully. "Perhaps Cardigan intended it as a gift for his sister."

"Twaddle! Would any sane man buy a toy like that for Miss Camellia? She'd no more use make up than you would."

"Still, it can't point to an affair of the heart—look at Peter Cardigan's age."

"As if that mattered! Put the thing in your pocket and start keeping a weather eye out for some frivolous lady who specializes in black and white trinkets."

Fisk slowly pocketed the vanity case, then went to examine the room's single window.

"I wonder if our murderer found what he wanted in the study or if he was scared off before he'd a chance to carry on here?"

"I think that window partially answers the question—it gives on the court and not the outer face of the building."

When they had exhausted the bed room's possibilities there seemed nothing more they could do that night, so the two men repaired to Traherne's bachelor establishment for a drink and a quiet discussion of the case.

"Comparing the various accounts of Peter Cardigan and his business, one rather gains an impression of something odd about his activities," was Traherne's first comment, delivered over the rim of a tall, cool drink. "The Cardigan maid's story of so many evening visitors who came almost by stealth—the singular shortage of papers in his office— his sister's tale of a quarrel serious enough to keep him walking the floor when he should have been in bed and asleep—and above all the effect of the black-bordered let- ter, or rather drawing, received at luncheon time. None of it quite falls into Kent Cardigan's picture of a conservative stock and bond firm."

"No," Fisk agreed. "And speaking of Kent Cardigan, do you think he knows more than he's told? Remember so far we've only his word that he was waiting in Schrafft's at the time of his father's death."

"We can tell better after the cashier he says he was talking to has been questioned. How do you feel about him?"

"A bit on the doubtful side, enough so that I've put a man on to shadow him though I hardly expect he'll leave home again tonight. Of course if the girl in Schrafft's backs his story that automatically lets him out as we've the camera's word for the time at which Peter Cardigan disappeared from that window."

"Yes, we know the hands of the Stanwix Bank clock pointed to the exact hour of three," Sydney Traherne assented, then ran worried fingers through his brindled black and silver hair until it stood rampant, lending him a wildly disheveled air. "What about that odd clause in Cardigan's will?"

"Meaning the safety deposit key that's not to be handed over until Kent's twenty-fifth birthday?"

"Naturally, what else? We're hardly concerned with the disposal of his body; once the coroner has rendered his verdict it's none of our business whether he's buried or cremated. But I can't shake off a feeling that the contents of that safety deposit box have some close connection with Peter Cardigan's murder."

"Yet how can they? The will was made six years ago when Kent was only nineteen."

"I know. All the same we must try to shake Mark Stanwix' determination not to anticipate Kent's birthday. Tomorrow would be much better than Wednesday for the opening of that box."

Before Fisk could answer the ringing of a bell called Traherne into the entrance foyer to answer it, and a second or two later he came back to say the inspector was wanted on the 'phone.

It was the man detailed to watch Kent Cardigan, calling to say that instead of remaining reasonably at home the son of the murdered man had waited until his aunt and the servants were in bed, then gone out to a night club; from which the operative was calling his chief to report. Fisk got the name and address of the club, then told his man to continue watching Kent's movements.

"We'll probably turn up there in, say, half an hour so keep an eye out for us."

He went back into Traherne's study and at once passed on the news of Kent Cardigan's surprising behavior.

"Why a night club of all places? If he'd gone to some woman friend or sweetheart for sympathy and advice you could understand it—but he must be a damned heartless young cub to go looking for excitement only a few hours after he'd heard of his father's murder."

"May have had an appointment which he felt compelled to keep." Traherne was prone to unexpectedly giving people the benefit of any possible doubt. "What type's the club he's gone to? Good, bad or indifferent?"

The inspector consulted his penciled note of its name and address. "It's called 'The Panther's Den.'—Never heard of it before, though that doesn't officially interest me unless somebody picks one to stage a murder. Shall we go and see if Kent Cardigan went there to meet anyone?"

"Right."

'The Panther's Den,' like many of its kind, was on the second floor of a building whose entire ground floor was taken up by innocent looking little shops of various kinds, most of them closed and darkened long before the night club woke to any real life. It was well over on the east side of town, not far from the river, and so tucked away amongst warehouses, cheap tenements and down-at-heel office buildings that few patrons unacquainted with its location would be likely to stumble upon it. Which perhaps accounted for the fact that the man on the street door made no difficulty about admitting Fisk and Traherne.

The big room onto which the narrow stairs opened directly was fantastically decorated to carry out the club's name of 'The Panther's Den.' In place of a ceiling was a papier-mâché imitation of the rocky roof of a huge cavern, from which suspended lamps designed in the form of stalactites, set at irregular intervals shed only sufficient light to carry out the illusion of an underground lair. The walls also closely simulated those of a natural cave, blending into the overhead rock that descended to meet them, while numerous buttress-like projections were so arranged as to form small recesses barely large enough to hold a single table; so securing a measure of privacy for such guests as desired it. On the tables themselves, both those set in the recesses and those nearer to the central dance floor, sat small, bizarre lamps shaped and colored like mushrooms of the more poisonous and hence more vividly colored varieties.

"Not badly done," was Traherne's approving comment as they took possession of a recessed table giving a fairly open view of the huge room. "After the modernistic decorations favored by most night clubs this weird semi-gloom comes as a distinct relief—though it's far from ideal for our own particular purpose. Can you see Kent Cardigan anywhere?"

"No, but we'll see more clearly once our eyes get accustomed to the dim light. So far I can't even see my own man."

By the time the waiter had taken their supper order and brought a preliminary drink Fisk's prediction touching their sight was verified and he was able to point out Kent Cardigan sitting alone at a table on the extreme edge of the dancing floor.

"No one's met him so far," the inspector drily observed. "Looks as if he was simply in quest of distraction."

"Why isn't he dancing then? A lot of those girls are surely club entertainers and they'd scarcely refuse a man with Kent's good looks."

"Here comes Rivers—perhaps he has something to tell."

But the operative who slipped quietly into the vacant place at their table could only report that so far Kent had shown not the slightest interest in anyone in the Panther's Den.

"Simply sat there and ordered one drink after another—looking all the time as if he was attending his own funeral," Rivers bitterly complained.

"Well, go back closer to the door and if he goes trail him," the inspector directed. "Don't come near us again unless you've something special to report."

As Rivers left them Sydney absently followed his unobtrusive progress toward the club entrance and he therefore noticed a newcomer whom he might otherwise have missed. For a split second he stared unbelievingly, then touched the inspector's arm.

"Look what just blew in!"

"Where?"

"At the main entrance."

It was the Stanwix butler, Fargo.

Seated where they were there was little chance of the man's seeing them, but they guessed by the care with which he avoided Kent Cardigan's vicinity that he had almost at once caught sight of the big blond man seated at his more conspicuous table.

Fargo sat down not far from the entrance, ordered a drink, and when it come sipped it slowly, seeming to pay no attention whatever to the people near him, or to the sprinkling of couples on the dance floor.

Presently Traherne saw him consult his watch, then rise and pass through a small arched opening inside which he could see one end of a row of telephone booths. From his place at the table Traherne was unable to see which one the butler entered, but by slightly shifting his chair he could keep the arched opening well in view and watch for the man's reappearance.

Meanwhile Kent Cardigan went on ordering and disposing of one drink after another with no visible effect, and their own supper arrived. The food was unexpectedly good and the lapse since dinner long enough to make it welcome, so that Traherne at first failed to realize how long Fargo remained in the telephone booth.

A couple of exhibition dancers completed their number, and Fisk and he finished their supper before the butler's continued absence began to really trouble him. Then he told Fisk he meant investigating and made his way toward the telephone arch, taking care to remain well aside from Kent Cardigan's direct line of vision.

There were six booths in all, arranged in a row along the side wall, and only one of them was occupied by a fluffy little lady busily talking—all the rest were empty and there was no sign whatever of Fargo though the room boasted no other door than the one through which Traherne himself had entered.

"Must have slipped out while you were watching that pair of fancy dancers," Conway Fisk declared when Traherne had returned to their table and told him of the butler's mysterious disappearance.

"No," Traherne unhesitatingly denied. "I kept an eye on that arch from the instant he passed through it until I followed his example."

"Then there must be another door."

"There's not," Traherne again contradicted. "The room's perfectly empty except for the row of phone booths and its walls are blank, plastered affairs where one couldn't possibly overlook a second door."

"Then he's still in one of the booths—maybe sitting down on the floor."

"Idiot!" Traherne grinned affectionately. "But as a matter of fact I looked inside all but the one the fluffy little lady was using—just on the chance that he'd fainted and fallen so he couldn't be seen through the glass upper half of the door."

"That's being thorough with a vengeance," the inspector jeered. "Look, Kent Cardigan is sitting up and taking notice."

Through the room's hot, liquor-scented air drifted sobbing minor notes that somehow suggested the far-off throbbing of tom-toms sounding through stifling tropic darkness, and the beat of naked black feet against uncovered earth. The place of the regular dance orchestra had been taken by six negroes garbed as slightly conventionalized African natives and playing only such savage instruments as properly belonged to the dark continent.

"Some special feature, this, and unless I'm much mistaken it's what Kent Cardigan came for."

In face of Kent's sudden alert interest in his surroundings Traherne could hardly disagree. They both watched as he shifted his chair slantwise to the table and leaned toward the dancing floor.

Instead of the amber spotlight that had flooded it during the previous number, a cold white ray cut through the Den's semi-gloom, and as the music loudened this odd white light rhythmically dimmed and brightened in time to its pulsing throb. The effect created was of something unreal, the three dancing figures that suddenly whirled out onto the floor seemed creatures imagined rather than actually seen.

Two superbly graceful negroes, tall, and lithe as the forest denizen for which the club was named, they wore only black hued furs and feathers of the jungle while in startling contrast the girl whose steps wove so perfectly with theirs was all in white; a silken costume that covered her from throat to ankle yet clung so closely to every supple curve of her small, exquisite body that when the white ray dimmed one caught the illusion of a lovely dancing nakedness.

Nowhere was there even a note of color, all black the men, all white the woman, save only for the midnight darkness of her tight-clipped hair like a smooth-fitting black cap, and her great dark eyes—even her lips carried no discord, they were creamed and powdered to match the dead whiteness of her face.

It was a dance wherein two males contended for the favor of the female—who cast her lure first for one, then the other, while the pulsing light that revealed, then obscured, robbed the fantasy of suggestion and lifted it into the realm of sheer artistry.

"Clever, all three of them," Inspector Fisk approved as the dance ended in the fall of one negro and the triumphant departure of the other bearing the slender white woman-shape on muscular, stiffly extended arms. "That girl ought to be starring on Broadway."

"Yes?" Traherne's eyes looked queerly introspective. "Odd coincidence—Kent's frank interest in a girl specializing in black and white."

"Coincidence?" the other echoed uncomprehendingly.

"Have you forgotten that enameled vanity case found in Peter Cardigan's bureau drawer?"

"Oh!" Fisk beckoned their hovering waiter as the three dancers took an encore then finally vanished, the white ray of light disappearing with them. "Who is that girl?"

"Our feature dancer, sir," the man answered on a note of personal pride.

"And her name?"

"Well, she's billed, and mostly spoken of as Mitzi Moore but—" he glanced half furtively about to be sure no one else was listening, "those in the know call her the Panther's Cub."

6

THE CHARRED FLAKE

"Oh, Inspector Fisk was rather a dear—it was the man with him I didn't like," Daphne Fane spoke with a meditative deliberation, as if mentally weighing her own reasons for objecting to Sydney Traherne.

"Why not?" Myron Stanwix' dark worshiping eyes were suddenly clouded; he dropped them to his breakfast plate, apparently conscious that they might tell too much. "He hardly spoke at all and seemed very little interested."

"Perhaps his very silence frightened me—it conveyed a sort of threat, as if he felt we were one and all suspicious characters needing to be closely watched. And then his eyes—" she shivered delicately, with an embarrassed smile, "did you notice how peculiar they are? Not a nice even color but striped, with little black rays fanning out from the pupils. They reminded me of cat's eyes!"

"Stop being insulting!" Faith Stanwix laughed at her. "My Tibit's eyes aren't a bit like that, are they darling!" She stooped to pick up a great sleek angora seated in majestic detachment between her own chair and Daphne Fane's. "See, his eyes are a lovely yellow that just matches his fur."

She tilted the animal's face toward her friend, and the round yellow eyes blinked with the superior, half pitying tolerance most cats seem to entertain for the entire human race. Glancing from his sister's pet to her friend,

Myron realized with a queer little premonitory chill, that the clear topaz of Daphne's eyes were identical, both in shade and shallowness, with those of the cat and vaguely wondered if she knew. He dared not ask and just then a diversion was created by the arrival of Murray Sanger.

"I came up to ask if there was any news," he explained, gratefully accepting Faith's offer of a cup of coffee though he admitted having breakfasted long ago, before his morning canter in the park.

"The inspector had a talk with daddy before any of the rest of us were awake," Faith informed him. "We were just discussing it, and the inspector himself, before you came in. Poor quiet old uncle Peter, it's so difficult to realize that he's suddenly become the center of all this excitement."

"I think some of us ought to go down and see what the police are doing in his office." Myron Stanwix nervously crushed the life out of his half-smoked cigarette and stood up. "Want to come along, Murray?"

"What's the use?" Sanger demurred. "We're none of us detectives, and besides they'd probably resent our interference."

"The inspector wouldn't," Daphne Fane spoke with a certain quiet conviction. "But as for that other man—watch out for him, I believe he's a naturally evil mind."

"Well, stay with the girls if you like. I'm going to the Cardigan office. Do you know if father's there, Faith?"

"Fargo told me he'd gone down to the bank," his sister answered. "But he talked over the phone to Kent before he left."

Murray Sanger finished the last of his coffee and rose with a quite obvious reluctance.

"All right, if you insist on horning in, old son, I'll trail—but I doubt our being in the least welcome."

They found Sydney Traherne and the inspector established in Peter Cardigan's private office with much of the
necessary routine questioning already behind them.

"We've gained very little new information," the inspector told the newcomers. "Most of the building's working
force have told what they know, and it's precious little."

"No suspicious characters seen hanging around Uncle
Peter's office on Saturday?" young Stanwix queried hopefully.

"Nary a one. The elevator boys on duty Saturday, both
on the office and apartment sides of the building, have
all been questioned—the boy, Paddy, corroborates your
incident of the exact time for his relief, by the way, Mr.
Sanger—and none of them can remember carrying any
suspicious strangers."

There was a little pause while Inspector Fisk shuffled
some papers on the desk before him, inwardly debating
whether to turn the visitors out or let them participate
in the next stages of the investigation. Apparently Myron
Stanwix read, or guessed, his thoughts, for he asked just a
trifle anxiously:

"Should Murray and I be in the way if we tucked ourselves in that corner and promised to be silent?"

"Quite the contrary," it was Sydney Traherne who unexpectedly answered. "Some point may come up on which
you'll be helpful and we're expecting your friend Kent
Cardigan any minute now."

The inspector let it go at that and when neither of them
asked as to Kent's present whereabouts volunteered the
information that he had gone. Accompanied by a detective, he was out to interview the cashier of Schrafft's
Fifty-eighth Street store, whose home address had been
furnished by the management as it was not her day on
morning duty.

"I only saw Uncle Peter's stenographer in the outer office as we came in," Myron Stanwix ventured. "What's become of his two outside salesmen?"

"Oh, one of them turned up on time this morning and both he and the stenographer say there was a large sum of cash in the safe when they left on Saturday. Somewhere between fifteen and twenty thousand that was paid in by a client too late for banking hours."

"Caesar!" For some reason young Stanwix welcomed the news with eager satisfaction. "Enough to supply a motive even for murder! How about the other salesman?"

"He'd planned starting this morning on an upstate trip through the smaller towns, so Mr. Cardigan's stenographer informs us. We've sent a man to his home in hopes of catching him before he actually leaves. Yes, come in," the last to someone who knocked on the communicating door between inner and outer office. It was one of the inspector's men to say that "Letty," the cleaning woman in charge of that particular block of offices was waiting outside.

"Bring her in," the inspector directed. "And see that we're not disturbed unless Kent Cardigan or the second salesman turns up—send either of them in at once."

Letty was a bedraggled, unprepossessing female of mature age, who sniffled into a dirty handkerchief and seemed more than half afraid of being personally accused of Peter Cardigan's murder.

"Mr. Cardigan was a nice, open-handed gentleman, and I hadn't nothing against him," she tearfully assured the men who had never for a moment supposed that she had.

"We'll take all that for granted," the inspector spoke with a bluff kindliness meant to put the woman at her ease. "Now, tell us anything that happened on Saturday— *anything,* remember, no matter how small."

Thus urged she earnestly tried to stir her torpid memory, producing: "I'm afraid nothing didn't happen at all, sir," as a first result.

"You came in here to clean as usual, didn't you?" He realized that any information she possessed would have to be more or less dragged from her piecemeal, and used the emptied trash baskets as a starting point.

"No, sir, I didn't," Letty informed him. "Us cleaning ladies come on at noon Saturdays 'stead of six o'clock like other days, and in here I'd only got as far as emptying the trash when Mr. Cardigan came back and shooed me out."

"Why was that?"

"He said he'd somebody very special coming to see him and didn't want me round stirring up dust."

"About what time should you say this happened?"

But fixing of a definite time was beyond Letty, the best she could do was be sure it was some time before the passing of the parade.

"Why didn't you come back later on in the afternoon, before you went off duty?"

"I wasn't neglectful, sir, honest I wasn't," Letty damply protested. "But what with Mr. Cardigan telling me not to clean, and me not seeing him or the strange gentleman leaving, I daren't come back."

"Strange gentleman! What strange gentleman?" the inspector almost barked at her.

"Oh, didn't I tell you I seen a stranger coming in Mr. Cardigan's office?"

"You did not! Describe him, what was he like and what time did he come in?"

"I don't know, sir," Letty was very meek about it, but hopelessly uninformative.

"Was it before or after the parade—at least you can remember that much."

After a good deal of slightly guilty hesitation she acknowledged it must have been before, because, after hanging from an upper window to watch the parade, she had not again returned to that floor.

"Do you know many of the building's tenants by sight?" Fisk finally inquired and was told that Letty "Hadn't noticed," most of them. "But you're fairly certain this man who entered Peter Cardigan's office was a stranger to you?" he insisted.

Yes, Letty was rather positive on that point though she found difficulty in explaining exactly why, at length deciding that it was because the man looked like a moving picture hero and wore a gray suit that had especially caught her fancy.

"Helpful description," Fisk complained when the cleaning woman had finally been dismissed. "A man wearing a gray suit and looking like a motion picture star! As if half the men in New York didn't favor gray for warm weather wear and Hollywood feature every possible, and impossible masculine type! We'll have to get help from some other quarter if we're to find this stranger who visited Peter Cardigan."

Here the 'phone rang and Traherne, who happened to be nearest it, answered.

"Someone for you, Fisk."

The inspector spoke briefly, listened at greater length, and turned to the others.

"Apparently the murderer didn't find what he'd been searching for in Peter Cardigan's study; that was headquarters calling to say his car was taken from its garage under a forged order from Mr. Cardigan at some time last night and has turned up this morning on a lonely by-road in Westchester with its cushions slashed to ribbons."

"Then the murderer's still after something of Uncle Peter's that he hasn't been able to find." Myron rather stated than asked.

"Obviously, and it must be a paper of some sort judging by the type of search he's conducted here, in Cardigan's study, and now in his car."

"Possibly it has to do with whatever dark secret lies stowed away in that mysterious safety deposit box," Traherne spoke with a careless, half casual laugh.

"Safety deposit? I haven't heard about that." Myron Stanwix glanced anxiously from one man to the other. "Is it a secret?"

"Oh quite. In fact I shouldn't have mentioned it except that I forgot you and Mr. Sanger weren't present last night when your father told of a clause in Mr. Cardigan's will stipulating that a certain private deposit box key must only be handed over to Kent Cardigan on his twenty-fifth birthday—supposing, of course, that his father departed this life before Kent reached that precise age."

"And the will doesn't say what's in the box?" Myron's clean cut dark face was alive with eager interest.

"Gives not the slightest hint."

"Who's to turn the key over to Kent?"

"That's also a point on which I'm ignorant."

"Here's Kent now," Murray Sanger interrupted.

Listening, they could all hear young Cardigan's pleasant deep voice in the outer office. He came in looking hot and rather worried.

"Sorry, inspector, but my alibi looks to be a bit of a flop; the Schrafft's cashier says she chats with so many people that she can't remember our little conversation at all."

"Unkind of her to let you know you'd made no impression, but it doesn't especially matter."

The next report that came in concerned Peter Cardigan's second bond salesman, a man named Roberts. The detective sent to his home in the hope of catching him before his departure on a scheduled two-week trip, reported that Roberts had started very early that morning,

telling his landlady that he meant going first to Troy, New
York and would like his mail forwarded to a certain hotel
in that city. As this information tallied with Roberts' itin-
erary as supplied by the dead man's stenographer, Inspector Fisk sent his man to Troy with directions to interview
Roberts at his hotel there and 'phone back if the salesman
was able to throw any light on Peter Cardigan's murder.

After a little more general talk Fisk made it plain to
the three inseparables that he and Traherne wanted to be
alone, and they reluctantly departed.

"Well?" He turned to his colleague with a questioning-
ly lifted eyebrow. "How about them?"

"What's your own opinion?" Traherne countered evenly.

"I'd like to know if Myron Stanwix is habitually a prey
to such jumpy nerves—even when his face muscles were
under control he had to put both hands in his pockets to
hide the fact that they wouldn't stay quiet."

"He's a neurotic type," the other condoned, adding:
"Don't you feel it would simplify matters to override Mark
Stanwix' insistence on abiding by the very letter of that
key-clause in Peter Cardigan's will?"

"I do. I've a growing suspicion that once that safety
deposit box is opened we'll know considerably more about
what the murderer's been searching for. In fact I've already
made an appointment with Mark Stanwix for this evening.
I'll be pretty well tied up with the inquest and following
stray clews the rest of the day, but by tonight he'll have
had time to realize that the situation's too serious to permit his stubbornly refusing to anticipate Kent's birthday
and handing over the key at once. You'll come up to the
bungalow with me, of course."

"No," Traherne refused. "I intend going back to the
Panther's Den, alone—and discovering what became of
our vanishing butler."

"Better take one of my men along. It's a bit risky poking into the club's private affairs on your own."

"Perhaps, but I prefer a lone hand—in an emergency it's never possible to tell what the other man may do. And by the bye, if we're to be in time for the inquest we ought to start along." He rose and strolled over to the washbasin set in a corner cabinet, standing near it while he pulled up his cuffs intending to wash his hands. The inspector was hastily collecting notebook and papers when a low: "Come here," from Traherne took him out of his chair and across the room in three long strides.

"Your men who searched here *could* have been a bit more thorough." Traherne was pointing to a blackened, water-soaked shred of paper that clung to the metal crosspiece an inch down the washbasin vent. "Someone's apparently burnt papers in this bowl and prudently washed the remains down the vent pipe."

With a cautious match he lifted out the charred flake, spreading it on his open palm where they could both examine it.

"Too far gone to give us even a word," there was keen disappointment in Fisk's tone.

"Yes, and I imagine that flake's all we'll ever see of the letter to Kent Cardigan that belonged in the envelope found by your men."

7

THE SCARED RABBIT

"Mr. Stanwix is waiting in the study, sir." As the elevator door closed behind Inspector Fisk, Fargo received him with the clock-like precision of the perfectly trained servant receiving an expected guest. Fisk watched him start down the hall, wondering if the man at all realized that he had attracted their attention. It was only at the study door that he paused, and after a second's hesitation, spoke slightly out of character:

"Beg pardon for detaining you, sir, but since hearing more about Mr. Cardigan's death it's occurred to me perhaps I ought to tell you he was very anxious to reach his son on Saturday afternoon; he telephoned here several times."

"Who answered the phone?"

"I did, sir, all three times. But I could only say Mr. Kent wasn't here and I'd no idea of his whereabouts."

"None of the family spoke to Mr. Cardigan?"

"They were none of them home, sir."

"He didn't say why he wanted to reach Kent?"

"No, sir. I only judged it must be for some important reason because he called three times and his voice sounded worried, anxious, if I may say so."

"Thanks. You were quite right to tell me, it may very well prove important."

Every new bit of evidence that came to light told against any easy theory of a mere robbery motive for Peter Cardigan's murder. His receipt of the black-bordered envelope at luncheon time on the day of his death and his subsequent anxiety to get into touch with his son strongly suggested that the old man had known himself in danger, and tried, too late as after events proved, to pass on some vital information—of what nature it was at present impossible to guess. Well, perhaps the contents of the safety deposit box would enlighten them; Mark Stanwix must be persuaded to consent to its opening.

The persuasion proved anything but an easy task, however. Stanwix was a stubborn, strong-willed man accustomed to his own way, who evinced an almost fanatic loyalty to the wishes of his dead friend and refused to be influenced even by Whitney Page's taking the inspector's side.

"Day after tomorrow is Kent's birthday—it can do no possible harm to delay opening the box until then," he insisted.

"But can't you understand the time element is always important in a murder investigation; sometimes hours are precious and the possession, or non-possession of certain facts may affect the entire case? Suppose that box contains the name of some enemy whom Cardigan greatly feared?"

"An enemy who remained inactive for almost six years? Remember the will was made when Kent was only nineteen."

"You can't be certain that the box contains the same secret now, as then," Fisk pointed out.

"I think the inspector's absolutely right, Mr. Stanwix," Whitney Page here took it upon himself to put in. "There's no telling how much, or in what way, the secret of that deposit box may help."

"Sorry, but I can't see it in that light," their host stiffly informed them. "Still, as I've no desire to be accused of retarding justice I'm willing to make a concession. Technically

Kent Cardigan reaches the age of twenty-five right after midnight tomorrow—well, if you care to have him here at that exact time I'll agree to handing over the key then, instead of at a reasonable hour on Wednesday morning which I think would be much more decent and fitting. Furthermore, I'll arrange to have certain men remain on duty at the bank tomorrow night so that the instant I give you, or rather Kent, the key you can all go down by way of the private elevator connecting this apartment with the bank, and immediately investigate the deposit box."

"It's not much, but it's something," Inspector Fisk conceded. "At least we save several hours' waiting. But this is the first I've heard of a strictly private elevator between the penthouse and the bank."

"When this building was put up a solid, nonstop elevator shaft between the two points was included in the plans and specifications," his host explained. "There's no secret about it, though possibly its existence is not generally known except, of course, to bank employees and my own family, because as it was designed solely for my own use and there are no stops on the way down, there's nothing about it to attract casual notice." Inspector Fisk made one last effort to hasten the delivery of the key and failing, agreed to Mark Stanwix' plan.

"One stipulation I'd like to make is that as few people as possible are told of our intention to meet here tomorrow night. In fact I'd suggest keeping it a strict secret and not even letting Kent Cardigan know what's going on."

"But in that case you'd risk not being able to reach him at the desired hour," Mr. Stanwix objected. "Though I think I see your point; you're afraid if the plan is too widely broadcast the murderer may attempt taking a hand."

"Exactly. To guard against interference, simply ask Kent to come here at, say, 11:30, as you've something to talk over with him."

"Very well."

The inspector said good-night and as he neared the hall door on his way out paused, with a suddenly puzzled look; there was a light, insistent scratching against the outer side of the wood. Half suspecting an eavesdropper he flung the door wide open, whereupon Faith's stately angora stalked sedately in, glanced briefly at the inspector, then around the room, and with a single pleased "meow" made for one of the heavily curtained rear windows.

"The animal belongs to my daughter," Mark Stanwix explained. "He's doubtless looking for her, or for Miss Fane, having developed a sudden marked devotion for Faith's new friend."

Unusual for a cat to come scratching on a closed door like that, Fisk reflected, more what one would expect from a dog. He absently watched the cat disappear behind the window curtains and then, moved by an impulse for which he could not himself quite account, went silently down the room and lifted one heavy curtain aside. On the broad windowseat behind it Daphne Fane lay curled up, to all appearances fast asleep, the big yellow cat sitting contentedly beside her.

Motioning the two men to silence, the inspector fished out the small, powerful electric torch he always carried and flashed its light close to Daphne's closed eyes; there was not the tiniest responding flicker of the silken fringed lids.

"She's asleep alright," Whitney Page whispered. "Wonder how long she's been there?"

"Since before we came in, of course, otherwise how could she have got there without our seeing her? That sill's too high for her to climb over and besides the window's shut."

"Were you here long before I came?" The inspector's rather heavy brows were knit into a perplexed frown.

"Perhaps twenty minutes, though I doubt its being quite so long," his host answered.

"And the room was apparently empty when you entered?"

"Yes." Then, with a sudden illumining flash of memory: "Come to think of it, Miss Fane complained at dinner of feeling sleepy; she must have come in here directly afterwards for a stolen nap."

"Let's wake her," Whitney Page suggested, his smooth white hand darting out to grasp Daphne's shoulder and gently shake it before either of the others could protest, had they been so minded.

She stirred softly, with a small abused murmur, then opened big golden eyes that looked misty with lingering filaments of scattered dreams.

"Oh! Was I asleep?" She sat up, blinking at the three men until Tibits, purring like a kettle on the boil, insinuated himself into her arms and absorbed most of her attention. "I didn't mean to," she smilingly apologized over the cat's furry head. "Bad manners, haven't we, Tibits dear, but I was *so* sleepy! I thought if I stole in here and rested for a little it might wear off. Has Faith been looking for me?"

"Not so far as I am aware," Mark Stanwix assured her.

"I must go and apologize." She left them, carrying the purring cat in her arms.

"Quite evident that she heard nothing," Whitney Page decided. "And if she did it would have no special meaning for her, we're all practically strangers."

The inspector seemed not quite satisfied but there was nothing he could do save accompany his host and Whitney Page out of the room.

When they had gone the big, luxurious study lay for perhaps five minutes bathed in the mellow glow of its overhead lights. Then a handkerchief-wrapped hand reached gently up from behind the shelter of a huge winged-back chair near the door, and, with a certainty of touch that vouched for steady nerve control behind it, flicked down the light switch, plunging the room in darkness.

As the evening was still fairly young Inspector Fisk drove to police headquarters instead of calling it a day and returning home. His subordinates reported no special news except that the man sent to Troy in the wake of the bond salesman, Roberts, had telephoned leaving a request for his chief to call him at a certain hotel in Troy at his earliest convenience. Fisk put through the necessary long distance and was presently listening to his operative's report.

"I'm not sure how much it means, but our man's behaving rather suspiciously," he told his chief. "He registered here this noon, telling the desk clerk he intended staying the best part of a week, sent a suitcase to the room assigned him and went directly out, carrying only a little briefcase in his hand. Well, he hasn't come back. I hung around all afternoon without getting suspicious. When he hadn't turned up at dinner time, I started getting anxious and made some inquiries. Found the taxi man from the hotel rank who took Roberts to a couple of business offices and was then paid off and dismissed. No one else seems to have seen Roberts at all and of course the business offices he went to closed long ago, so can't be got at until morning."

"That's all you've learned?"

"Practically. Except the taxi man says Roberts left a couple of this morning's New York papers in his car."

"Humph. Well, stay on the job and let me hear, instantly, if you pick up Roberts' trail."

Not so good, the inspector told himself, it looked as though Roberts had read the newspaper accounts of Peter Cardigan's murder and promptly bolted. Why? The natural action of any responsible salesman of a reputable firm on hearing that his employer had been murdered would probably be an instant return to the head office; instead of which the news seemed to have sent Roberts bolting like a scared rabbit; he had even abandoned his suitcase left at the hotel.

Not the murderer himself, evidently, else the news would have caused him no surprise. Did he hold incriminating evidence against the guilty person or was some already half guessed irregularity about the business itself responsible? And, reflecting on possible business irregularities, was a suspicion of something of the sort and consequent desire to shield his old friend's memory, the motive behind Mark Stanwix' stubborn objection to premature opening of the safety deposit box? Did he, perhaps, either know or strongly suspect more concerning its contents than he had been willing to acknowledge?

Well, another twenty-four hours or more the box would have given up its secret; Inspector Fisk could only fervently hope that it would cast some light on the Stygian darkness surrounding Peter Cardigan's murder.

8

"Not Drunk—In Love!"

Before the days of successful playwrighting Sydney Traherne had served several years of apprenticeship to the stage as a character actor, and held decided views on the matter of make-up and impersonation, both for the stage itself and for such times as he bent his energies toward crime detection.

In making ready for his solitary venture into the Panther's Den he used only the barest touch of carefully applied grease paint to give the impression of a face flushed by too free indulgence in alcohol, very slightly changed and lengthened the natural line of his eyebrows, and parted his hair in the direct center instead of combing it straight back; thereby accomplishing a marked alteration in his appearance while still eschewing any disguise that need fear even a strong light.

Well cut but rumpled evening clothes and a silk hat showing two or three recently acquired dents completed his preparations for the part of a man who had dined not wisely but too well.

Traherne waited until a little after twelve before taking a taxi to the night club which would by that time, he imagined, be well enough filled to permit of one more inebriated gentleman's unobtrusively blending into the general background.

On reaching the big upstairs supper room he found it much more crowded than on the previous night, so that he was unable to get a table quite as close to the archway leading to the telephone booths as he would have liked, though a small vacant table gave him a slanting view including most of them.

Once seated it was only a question of remaining on watch until someone entered the telephone room and in the meantime, behaving in such a way as to attract no attention for if his half formed suspicions regarding the Panther's Den were accurate, all the waiters probably had orders to keep an eye out for any strangers showing an undue curiosity about the club's private affairs.

He ordered a bottle of wine and some food, then settled down to watch. For an hour or more nothing happened save a few false alarms when one patron or another went in to telephone and having done so, came directly out again. Then, after the Panther Cub's special number was finished and Traherne's patience had begun to wear a trifle thin, a beautifully gowned woman supping with a hilarious party of friends rose and, murmuring some excuse, drifted casually through the arch. He saw her enter the second of the telephone booths—a slanting view of the door to which could be had from where he sat—and thereafter she failed to reappear. One of her party, a man, finally grew impatient and wove a staggering way to investigate, failed to find the lady and returned to their table where he proceeded to drown his disappointment as rapidly as possible.

Next a dignified elderly gentleman used the same booth and likewise vanished, not to reappear.

Sure, by now, that the second telephone booth masked some private exit from the room beyond the arch, Traherne concluded he must change to a table commanding a better view of it, and looked about for an inconspicuous method of accomplishing the move.

At an ideally situated table two girls whom he guessed
as employees of the night club were having supper, fa-
miliarly chaffing the waiter who served it in a way that
confirmed Traherne's previous belief that they belonged to
the personnel of the Panther's Den. Risking the accuracy
of his guess he ordered another bottle and when it arrived, waved it invitingly toward the two girls, at the same
time pantomiming a burning desire to share it with them.
Encouragement to wine-ordering patrons being part of
their job, they signaled back permission to join them.

From his new position between the two laughing girls
Traherne could not only see the second telephone booth
clearly, but could also catch a fairly comprehensive view
of its interior, and elatedly felt himself well on the road
to discovering what had become of the Stanwix' vanishing
butler; that is, if any more of the initiated used the secret
exit.

For some little time no one did, then a quietly dressed
man entered the supper room and without pausing at any
of the tables made direct for the second booth. Over a
bobbed girlish head now affectionately reposing against
his shoulder, Traherne saw him enter the booth, drop a
coin into its slot and then, instead of taking down the re-
ceiver, seize the metal arm holding the telephone mouth-
piece twist it sharply to the left and thereafter instantly
disappear from view. While he had not actually seen the
booth back open, door-wise, it was obvious that that was
what must have happened. It remained only to get rid of
the girls so that he might personally investigate the trick
telephone booth.

Realistic portrayal of the various stages from hilarious
good fellowship to a quarrelsome desire for trouble, any
sort of trouble with those about him, being included in
the repertoire of most character actors, Traherne promptly began practicing this unforgotten lore and quite easily

succeeded in driving the girls into seeking a better tempered and more generous host.

After their desertion he slumped across the table apparently overcome by sleep, but sufficiently recovered when a too attentive waiter aroused him, to order still another bottle as an excuse for not wearing out his welcome.

The Panther's Den seemed altogether embarrassingly well supplied with waiters, but watching a chance when they were none of them in the immediate vicinity, he rose on unsteady feet and wavered in through the arch, slipped inside the second booth, and, closely following the gestures made by its last occupant, was rewarded by seeing the back wall swing inward showing only a gapping blackness beyond.

Well aware of the risk he was taking, Traherne slid through the opening and let the false booth-back snap back into place, then stood perfectly quiet, not daring to use the electric torch he had brought along.

The dead closeness of the air told him he was in some inner room, a place so dark that even when his pupils had gained their fullest expansion he was still unable to discern anything of his surroundings.

Deprived of the use of eyes, hands must be made to serve; he groped a cautious way through the blackness, devoutly trusting that no collision with unseen furniture would give the alarm. His outstretched fingers at length encountered a wall, and, following it, an unlocked door. Once through that felt rather than saw he was in a bare passageway cutting off at an angle from the supper room he had recently left.

A brief reconnoiter showed that passageway as a bad place in which to be caught prying, for it lacked any sort of cover. He padded briskly, but soft-footed down its length to where it branched, one turn giving on a line of closed doors, the other blocked by a stairway climbing to the floor above.

There was no one in sight, no sound of voices; should he venture into the dead-end, dimly lighted passage and listen outside those closed doors, or try the stairs? While he hesitated decision was taken from him by muffled footsteps approaching from the direction of the main supper room; Traherne shot round the angle of the wall and went up the stairs like a cat up a tree.

From the shelter of the upper hall he listened as the steps shuffled slowly along and stopped; there was the rattling of a key, then a door closed and he guessed the owner of the footsteps had opened one of those shut doors in the long passageway.

Relieved from fear of immediate discovery Traherne bent all his energies to the task of intent listening. After all those three whom he had personally seen use the trick booth as a means of access to this part of the building must have done so for some reason; must in all likelihood be still here, he had only to find them and whoever they had come to see, in order to gain at least a partial knowledge of the inner workings of the Panther's Den.

Always gifted with more than averagely keen hearing, once he had quieted the pounding of blood in his own ears Traherne was able to catch a faint murmur of distant voices and following the sound, presently found himself caught in a labyrinth of short halls and small, ill-lighted rooms, which seemed to fairly honeycomb this entire upper floor. Twice he narrowly missed being seen by men suddenly emerging from nearby doorways, but each time gained a recess or wall-angle in time to avoid discovery and began to feel, with a certain thrill of adventurous elation, that luck was with him; he would eventually find what he sought.

Once he took some wrong turning and completely lost the guiding murmur of voices, but when he next picked it up the sound was much nearer, so near in fact, that he silently dropped to all fours and crept forward until a turn in the dim passageway showed him a knife-like strip of light that filtered between the leaves of swinging doors. He reached them and, lying prone on the carpetless floor, pushed one leaf ever so gently, applying a cautious eye to the thus widened crack.

Inside was a bare, comfortless room furnished only with a few rough deal tables and numerous hard wooden chairs, many of them occupied by the strangest assortment of people, perhaps a dozen or fifteen in all.

From his strategic position on the floor—chosen because the tell-tale gleam of a human eye catching reflected light would be much less likely to attract notice at that level than at a more normal height—Traherne's field of vision gave an undue prominence to the companies lower extremities, yet even allowing for that distortion of viewpoint they were a motley crew.

Among them was the beautifully gowned woman whom he had seen leave her party of friends, and a thin, painted girl of an unmistakable profession; all the rest were men. Several of them bore every earmark of the well born and well bred New Yorker; others resembled the more flashy type of racing men; two were unshaven and frankly dirty; another wore clerical garb that to Traherne's trained eyes smacked more of a theatrical costume than the authentic cloth of the Church. A few seemed foreigners, probably of some Latin race, but the majority were American and whatever else might be said of them, there was not one face there that lacked a keen, alert intelligence.

Apparently no class distinctions were observed in this strange gathering for the little painted prostitute sat at one table with the man dressed as a minister and three most correctly attired gentlemen, while the beautifully gowned woman, the dirtiest of the two unshaven tramps, and four or five of the violently tailored and jeweled sporting men made up a second table.

It was the murmur of betting, raising, calling, incidental to a poker game, together with desultory conversations carried on while the cards were being shuffled and dealt that drifted out for Traherne's guidance.

As he watched the little prostitute raked in a pot, smothered an incipient yawn, and while the man next her was shuffling, bent over and asked for the time.

"Just on 2:30," somebody answered.

"Hell!" her nasal voice held sharp indignation. "What does the Panther think we are? Owls? Pity he wouldn't wise up that we've all got homes."

"Shut up," one of her companions sharply advised. "If there's one thing he won't stand for it's crabbing. Look what happened Flopsey-May."

"Ya." The girl struggled for a defiant note but Traherne saw her shiver as she picked up her just dealt hand and she offered no more comments on the lateness of the hour.

For a time nothing was heard but the clink or rustle of staked money and the clipped sentences of poker jargon; while Traherne unhappily meditated on the strong probability of this man whom they called the Panther suddenly arriving and stumbling over his prostrate body. Then the expensively gowned woman spoke to the room at large and he promptly forgot his own danger in the interest of what she said.

"Anybody know what's caused the excitement? It's not like him to get the wind up and send a hurry call for so many of us unless there's something serious; this isn't a regular meeting night, you know."

"Trust a woman to everlastingly trot out her curiosity and growl—first Jenny and now you!" The man who had warned the little prostitute against talking threw down his cards with a stifled oath. "What's it to do with you what he wants? We're here to take the Panther's orders, ain't we? Not to ask questions!"

"I wasn't crabbing," the woman tranquilly pointed out. "Only wondering why he wants us—"

"Well, if you take my tip you'll close that pretty mouth of yours instead." He favored her with a baleful glare. "He pays, don't he? It's up to him to sic us or leash us as best fits his cards."

"Maybe the Panther's pet cub has been playing round," Jenny spitefully suggested and was promptly sworn at for her pains.

"Oh, for God's sake shut up! How do you know the Panther ain't listening in?"

The effect of his words spoke volumes for the discipline maintained by their chief; there was an instant hush and a restless movement which included even the men sitting away from the card tables, who had taken no part whatever in the conversation overheard by Traherne.

Through this suddenly complete silence came a small muffled click, like the snapping back of some well-oiled bolt and at the sound, slight as it was, everybody in the room shifted position, abandoning the card tables and all moving back to cluster against the rear wall of the room where Traherne could no longer see them.

What was happening? Unless the wall to the right of the door held another opening hidden from his present position, no one had entered; then why the coordinated move to the back of the bare room and the breathless, waiting silence?

As he racked his brain for an answer a new voice spoke, or rather whispered; an eerie, muted voice utterly sexless and without personality. To save his life Traherne could not have told if it was the voice of a man, or a woman. How was it managed, he wondered, how that lifeless, metallic effect obtained? Then, as the voice went on he guessed that someone, man or woman, was softly whispering through a megaphone. Clever idea, it completely robbed the voice of any recognizable quality so that even his own followers would never know it, if heard in its natural tones. Was, then, the Panther's identity a secret even from his own men?

The thin metallic whisper went on to inform the listening group that certain unspecified events had caused a modification of previous plans; some of them were to receive new instructions.

The unseen Panther called a name and the man wearing clerical garb left the rear wall, crossed Traherne's field of vision and passed out of its limits toward the right wall; then the listener savored keen disappointment for the whispering voice sank so low that he could distinguish nothing it said.

For a moment he lay quite still, fighting an utterly mad impulse to crawl into the room and closer to that eerie, muted voice, then he let the door's leaf swing shut, squirmed silently around until his head pointed in the opposite direction than before, and, only a hair's breadth at a time, eased open the leaf hitherto left undisturbed.

Now he could see the room's right wall which at first glance looked completely blank, and the black-garbed figure standing a couple of feet from it; no one else in sight. Only when he looked more closely did Traherne realize that the whispering murmur of directions came from behind a fancifully scrolled grill set into the wall at about the height of a man's head from the floor and painted a dull drab of precisely the same shade as the wall itself. To a casual eye the thing looked like an old fashioned hot-air register, and would most probably have escaped attracting attention from the uninitiated even had the room been searched, yet it excellently served its purpose. Whoever stood in the dark behind it would be perfectly invisible to the room's occupants unless they actually pressed their face against the swirling scrolls.

While Traherne watched the man in ministerial dress went back to join the others and in answer to a name he failed to catch, the beautifully gowned woman took his place near the grill. Followed more indistinguishable directions and then another name.

"Andre."

In answer one of the foreigners approached the grill; a dark, lithely built man with a clever, unscrupulous face. He seemed chosen for some especially important task requiring explicit directions for the whispering voice went on and on, ending with the appearance of a tiny, black-wrapped bundle thrust out through the grill. Andre reached for it, bungled because of nervousness or fright, and the wrapping came undone so that Traherne saw an inch-square bit of bright yellow silk float down to the floor. The foreigner scrambled to rescue it and from behind the grill came a single sibilant sentence laden with furious venom.

After that small incident the rest of the group by the wall came forward, one by one, got their orders and went back. The night's proceedings seemed ended, there was a repetition of the muffled click and several audible sighs of relief from the group as they commenced scattering, some returning to the poker tables to pick up their neglected winnings, others collecting hats or various small belongings; then someone hurrying along the darkened hall stepped on Traherne and everything happened at once.

A startled oath, the thud of a crashing blow, a heavy body landing against the wall, and light-running feet that fled precipitately—the pack that tumbled pell-mell out of the room of the grill in full cry.

Taking full advantage of the few seconds respite gained by the blow which had knocked the man who stepped on him momentarily out of the running, Traherne tried to lose himself in the labyrinth of small rooms and passageways, but the pursuit was anything but noiseless, the whole upper floor seemed to have burst into violent turmoil and people attracted by the hub-bub kept unexpectedly popping around corners and out of doors. It was too dark to see clearly, and besides none of them knew what was wrong; Traherne successfully dodged between two men before they could sufficiently gather their wits to grapple, shook off another with a backhanded swipe that sent him spinning, but the main pack were spreading out and calling as they came, some of them were already between him and the stairs leading down to the main floor.

Well, if escape was cut off in the way he had come—there remained the as yet unexplored upper regions. He hunted another stairway, found it, and darted up.

For a little he hoped the pursuit had been shaken off but either someone had caught a distant view of his flight up the stairs or the pack had simply guessed his line of retreat—he could hear them noisily searching the upper floor. Was it the top one, and what sort of possibilities did the roof hold out?

The place seemed to boast no skylights, or at least for several minutes he could discover none, then he unexpectedly came on a second, or third stairway, he was not sure which, leading steeply down to the floor he had left. Almost directly above it was an open skylight and a kind of ladderlike contraption pulled up flush with the ceiling. Working quickly he let the thing down then, just as men's voices called to each other only a short distance away, bestrode the stair's banister and slithered down.

Not until too late did he hear a door open and see a shaft of brilliant light cutting the darkness of the lower hall—he struggled to check his own momentum, failed, but succeeded in bouncing clear over the banister's low newel post to land with a resounding thump, ignominiously seated full in the shaft of light from the open door.

"Well! Are you the cause of all that infernal din?"

It was the black and white girl of the jungle specialty who had been standing outside the fan of light and at his abrupt arrival stepped over its rim. Traherne merely nodded blandly—not yet sure of his best line.

"But why? What have you been doing?"

"Only looking for you!" His infatuated grin was a masterpiece of sheer idiocy.

She came closer, suspicion in the big black eyes that intently studied his face.

"Is that the truth?"

"Course it's the truth!" He beamed at her benignly without making the smallest motion to get up or otherwise remove himself from that betraying blaze of light, though he could catch distant echoes of the chase which had evidently followed his false lead up on to the roof. "Saw you first time las' night—friend wouldn't let me stay—came back tonight!" He stopped, apparently considering everything explained.

The girl's supple body suddenly bent over him, nose frankly sniffing at his lips; Traherne inwardly thanked God for those unwanted bottles he had consumed in the interest of character-atmosphere.

"You're drunk."

She straightened and stood looking down at him while the noise from the roof increased and his heart felt as if it climbed up into his mouth and sat down, hard, on the root of his tongue.

"No, not drunk," he reproachfully informed the girl. "In love!"

"Ha! Much the Panther'll care for that if he catches you! Give me the truth now—have you seen or heard anything out of the ordinary—interesting?"

"Tell you I couldn't find you," he seemed able to harp only on that one string. "Hunted acres of rooms, miles of halls—you not anywhere! Got so tired I went to sleep and somebody stepped on me—that started all the row."

"Poor devil! The Panther'll never believe— Come, I'll hide you."

With a strength surprising in such a small slender thing she almost dragged him to his feet and into the lighted room, softly closing the door behind them.

9

Stabbed

"Your friend is not with you tonight!" Mark Stanwix signed the inspector to a nearby chair while Fargo solicitously proffered a tray containing the necessary ingredients for whisky, or brandy and soda.

"No." Fisk helped himself to the latter and waited until the butler had left the room before continuing. "Mr. Traherne drove to New Haven this afternoon. It's not yet generally known, but Peter Cardigan's salesman, Roberts, was found dead there today. Traherne went to see if it was an accident as reported by the local authorities or—murder."

"God!" The hand holding Stanwix' glass trembled so that he was obliged to set down his drink. "You think his death's in some way connected with Peter's?"

"We're not sure. Still the man's sudden flight when he learned of his employer's death suggests that he feared some personal danger, or else that he possessed guilty knowledge concerning the crime. After he disappeared from Troy my man was unable to get on his trail, in fact the next we heard of him was that he lay dead in New Haven, the victim of a traffic accident. Since I couldn't go myself Sydney Traherne went to investigate."

"You've not heard what he discovered?"

"No more than a hint. He 'phoned early this evening, he was starting back then, and mentioned certain evidence

better told in person than over the 'phone." A worried
frown puckered the inspector's wide forehead as he consulted his own watch, then glanced at the grandfather clock
near the fireplace. "It's eleven thirty-five. I don't understand his not being here by now. After all New Haven's not
such a tremendous distance away and when Traherne's in a
hurry he drives like an inspired demon."

"You arranged to have him come directly here?"

"Not originally. We were to have met at his apartment
but when he hadn't turned up at 11:20 I came on to keep
our appointment, leaving word with his man for Traherne
to follow. What makes me anxious is that only something
pretty serious could keep him away when that devilish
key's handed over to Kent Cardigan."

"Engine or tire trouble, perhaps," his host offered com-
fortingly.

"Perhaps. All the same I'd be glad to know where he is."

There was a little silence in the room, broken only by
the soft tinkle of ice in their glasses and the slithering rustle of silk curtains blown by a strengthening breeze.

"Kent Cardigan is here? In the bungalow I mean?" Fisk
at length inquired.

"Yes. Since we decided on keeping our plan more or
less secret I simply asked Faith to invite Kent here for the
evening, and to see that he didn't leave before we had a
little talk. Whitney Page went to the music room to get
him just before you came. They'll be back any minute now.

"And you've arranged about our visit to the bank's safe
deposit vault as soon as Kent has the key?"

"Yes. There are three men on duty besides the ordinary
nightwatchman. They understand what's wanted, though I
intend going down with you myself."

Here Whitney Page's voice, lifted in a plaintively pro-
testing wail, was heard in the hall. The door opened and
he came in, closely followed by the three inseparables.

"I've explained that we only want Kent!" His plump white hands thrown out in a deprecating gesture. "But he insisted on bringing the others along."

"Sorry." Stanwix glanced at the clock which showed eight minutes to twelve. "Mr. Page is quite right. We want a private conference with Kent."

"Come on, old dear, that's our exit cue." Murray Sanger's engaging smile quirked his eyebrows into even more acute points than nature intended. "Ghastly bad manners to outstay our welcome." He linked a persuasive arm through Myron Stanwix', edging him toward the door.

"No!" Kent seemed to look on their departure in the light of a desertion, there was distinct reproach in his voice as he went on: "After our talk this afternoon the least you can do is stick by me."

"H-um—fears we mean putting him on the grill, or maybe accusing him of his father's murder," was the thought that flashed through Inspector Fisk's mind.

"Oh, if you put it like that of course we'll stick!" Sanger calmly established himself in the nearest chair with the air of one whom it would require nothing short of physical violence to remove. "After all, nobody ever did accuse me of having decent manners."

"But I tell you you're not wanted!" Mark Stanwix glared belligerently first at the sweetly unruffled Sanger, then at his own son.

"Either they stay or I go with them," Kent issued his ultimatum.

"Ah, in that case—" Another glance assured Stanwix that it now lacked only four minutes to midnight. If he was to keep his word and hand over the key on the stroke of twelve there was no time to waste on getting rid of the group's two unnecessary members, besides their inclusion hardly mattered and Kent showed every sign of waxing stubborn on the point. He let it drop and rapidly sketched his decision to give Kent the key so specifically mentioned in his father's will, at the very earliest instant compatible with the strict observance of the clause concerning it.

"Inspector Fisk plans taking you down to the bank vault immediately afterward," he finished, eyes on the clock and the safety deposit key already in his hand.

As the clock's first booming note commenced tolling midnight, he laid the key on Kent's open palm, stretched to receive it.

"The utmost concession I could make—"

Mark Stanwix' voice died in his throat as every light in the room went suddenly out—leaving a velvety blackness through which the clock's resonant, unhurried notes continued to strike the hour.

There was the soft crash of some small object falling to the heavy-plied carpet—confused movements—disjointed ejaculations—a half stifled oath. Then a choking, agonized cry that was almost a scream.

Still the unheeding clock went on, ten, eleven, twelve— the cessation of its measured clamor came as blessed relief; also they were beginning to recover from the first numbing shock of unexpected darkness. Somebody called a question, somebody else in trying to light a lamp rather felt than seen succeeded in upsetting it, adding the splintering clatter of broken glass to the room's muffled uproar.

Murray Sanger found his cigarette lighter and by its tiny flame they found themselves huddled unexpectedly close—eyes glaring violently into others, half seen eyes, breath coming in uneven jerks.

"Beg pardon, sir, but all the lights have gone out. I thought I'd best bring a lamp." Fargo's tranquil voice spoke from somewhere in the neighborhood of the door which no one afterward could remember having heard open.

"Then why in hell don't you light it? You blithering idiot!" Mark Stanwix furiously barked at him.

"Sorry, sir, but I can't seem to find a match."

Inspector Fisk supplied one and next instant the lamp-wick's uncertain flame as it caught and steadied, dispelled the worst of that nightmare darkness—dispelled it, only to show them a new, more awful horror; fallen back across the heavy table Kent Cardigan lay with white upturned face and crimsoned hands clutching his breast. Even as their incredulous eyes fixed on those hideously reddened fingers a convulsive shudder ran through the big, awkwardly stretched frame, then it settled to unmoving rigidity on the thick rug.

"Christ—he's dead!"

Forgetful of everything but the swooping death that had struck there, almost under their eyes, Conway Fisk pulled at the clutching hands that limply obeyed his touch; under them was a slash in Kent's dinner coat and a stain that widened and spread to the white of his shirt.

"Stabbed!" He straightened, an uneven pallor mottling his face. "Let no one leave this room—the murderer is here!"

"But the knife? What's become of the knife?" Myron's voice was high and thin, touching the verge of hysteria.

"Fall back, all of you," Fisk ordered harshly. "Over there by the mantel—you've all got to be searched." He glanced almost helplessly about, seeking someone whom he could trust, then caught at the desk 'phone. "Headquarters—yes—Inspector Fisk of the Homicide Bureau speaking." The call was put through in record time and he was giving orders for men, and expert electricians, to be rushed to his aid.

"Those lights going out when they did was no accident," he addressed no one in particular, seeming to regard them all with an equal suspicion. Then to Fargo, who still stood nearest the door. "Don't let them in!"

He had caught the flutter of feminine garments, but too late to prevent their owner's entry, Faith and Daphne Fane were in the room tearfully demanding to be told what had happened and what was wrong with the lights.

"Murder, that's all!" His usual kindliness was buried under accumulated woes; first news of the salesman's death, then keen anxiety over the non-appearance of his friend, and now this crowning outrage—a man stabbed to death within three feet or so of where he himself stood. And he had liked big, blond Kent Cardigan. He felt his murder as something in the nature of a personal affront.

"Now," there was a rasp in his normally pleasant voice. "You'll every last one of you give a detailed account of what happened when the lights went out. Stop crying, Miss Stanwix," this last to Faith, who was softly sobbing in the shelter of Daphne's arms. "You, and your friend sit down on that sofa by the window—now you've forced your way in you'll have to stay. Nobody leaves the room till that knife is found."

"And the key! Where's the key?" It was Whitney Page who, with the question, darted toward Kent's body bent on looking to see if the key was still in his hand.

"No." The inspector jerked the little man back and almost threw him toward the group by the mantel. "None of you goes near the body while I'm alone with you—we'll look for the key later, it can't have flown away. Now, Mr. Stanwix," his tone was crisply business like, "you were nearest Kent Cardigan when the lights went out, give me your version of what happened."

"Why—nothing, nothing definite, that is," Mark Stanwix' manner had lost every trace of its normal rather dictatorial surety. "Someone brushed against me, I thought at the time it was Kent."

"And you yourself, what did you do?"

"I think I stepped back a little; one would be apt to try avoiding a collision in the dark."

"Now," the inspector went a little closer to him, "this person who brushed against you—what impression did you get from the contact? Was there any sense of violence, was the unseen person hurrying toward, or away, from where Kent stood when you gave him the key?"

"I'm not at all sure; but no, the thought of violence never occurred to me, it was more the light brushing of someone's coat sleeve against mine."

"You heard no struggle?"

"No."

"Any word spoken by Kent himself?"

"No."

"Surely you didn't simply stand still there by the table, you must have said or done *something.*"

"I tried to find the table lamp. It was the overhead lights that had gone out, I thought the lower lamps might be on a different fuse."

"Was it you who upset the one over there?" Fisk pointed to a fallen bridge-lamp, the shattered glass of its shade winking evilly in the uncertain light.

"I did that," Whitney Page volunteered. "The beastly thing was topheavy and fell when I tried to turn it on."

"Thanks. One more question, Mr. Stanwix, can you swear you heard no scuffle, no loud breathing, close to you just before Kent cried out?"

"Breathing, yes, the room seemed full of men almost panting—doubtless the darkness exaggerated my sense of hearing—but no sound suggesting a scuffle."

"Oh, for pity's sake throw something over Kent! Don't leave him like that—where we can't help seeing all that dreadful blood!" Faith besought, unable to suppress her own mounting horror.

"Sorry. You shouldn't have insisted on coming in when you heard me tell Fargo not to let you. The body has to be left undisturbed until the medical examiner gets here."

"Oh, cruel! I can't bear it, I can't bear it!"

She cowered close to the couch back, face pressed hard against a pillow, but Daphne Fane's great golden eyes, more than ever like the eyes of a cat, steadily watched every smallest move, every changing expression, of the men grouped under the inspector's accusing glare.

He turned next to the dapper little lawyer. "Now, Mr. Page, besides upsetting the lamp, what else did you do while the room was dark?"

"Mostly tried to keep out of everybody's way," Whitney Page decided after a little careful thought. "The rest of you are all so much bigger than I am—and it seemed that none of you stayed still, the room was full of confused movement."

"Any of it center around Kent Cardigan?"

"That I can't tell you."

"Yet when the room went dark you were standing pretty close to him."

"Was I? I fear my memory of the details is a trifle blurred. What stands out most clearly is the horrid voice of the clock—in the darkness it sounded like hammer blows on a giant gong."

"Yes." Fisk nodded with a touch of sympathy. "It seemed to intend going on forever. So you can't remember hearing, or feeling, anyone moving close to young Kent?"

"Sorry, but what few thoughts I had aside from dodging people and listening to that clock, were concentrated on trying to find a lamp."

"So." The Inspector turned next to Murray Sanger. "How about you, Mr. Sanger? Any helpful information to offer?"

"'Fraid not. Somebody trod on my toe and somebody else grabbed my elbow just a second after the lights died— but I've no idea who either of them was."

"Could either have been Kent Cardigan?"

"Hardly. If you remember I was sitting in that chair over there, I stood up almost at once but he was too far away to have touched me, I think, though of course it's difficult to be certain in the dark. "

"One moment, inspector!" Whitney Page had suddenly commenced excitedly fidgeting. "Have you noticed the electric torch under the table?"

"It happens to be mine," Fisk nodded. "I always carry one but tonight, when its light might have prevented murder, it refused to work; in struggling with its catch I dropped it."

"Oh, I just wondered how it came there." Page meekly subsided.

"Now, Mr. Sanger, can you say if anyone passed you hurrying toward, or away from where Kent Cardigan stood?" the inspector resumed his cross questioning.

Sanger considered very carefully before answering: "I daren't say for certain, but I've retained an impression of someone's passing me rapidly, almost on a run in fact; whoever it was seemed headed away from the big table going more or less over there."

He waved a slightly vague hand and following its general direction the inspector's eyes alighted on Fargo.

"So—in other words somebody fled past you toward the door leading into the hall."

10

The Human Agency

"When Kent Cardigan insisted on your remaining here he spoke of a talk you'd had this afternoon. What was it about?"

Having extracted all the information Sanger seemed able to impart, the inspector passed on to Myron Stanwix.

"I'd rather not say, it was of a strictly confidential nature." Myron's clean-cut face looked pinched and haggard in the lamp's wavering light.

"Don't you think his murder removes any bar to passing on its content?"

"Perhaps. I'd like knowing Murray's opinion."

"We ought to help the police in every possible way," Sanger gave it without waiting for a direct question.

"Even to the extent of telling about that letter?" Myron insisted on his friend's fully sharing the responsibility.

"To *any* extent."

"Then—well, we three had a talk this afternoon and Kent confessed to being worried for fear you suspected him of his father's murder," Myron spoke with a certain breathless rapidity hinting at suppressed excitement. "He'd read the police always looked first for motive and opportunity and of course he stood to benefit financially by his father's death, also he had no real alibi for the Schrafft's cashier didn't remember talking with him and he'd no way of proving he hadn't actually just left Mr. Cardigan's office when the watchman met him going down stairs. That angle worried him a lot and on top of that he'd received a mysteriously threatening letter in the morning's mail."

"What sort of threat?" the inspector cut in as Myron paused for breath.

"We both read it; only a line or two printed in an obviously disguised hand. It warned him against using 'the key' when it was given to him and was signed with a queer little drawing instead of a name."

"You don't remember the exact wording?"

"No more than I've already told you."

"Could either of you reproduce this drawing that was used in place of a signature?"

The question included Sanger and it was he who first answered it in the negative.

"I was always a dub at sketching; the thing's clear enough in my memory but I couldn't draw it to save my life."

"Or say what it was meant to represent?"

"Some kind of an animal. I'd hate guessing the exact species."

Myron Stanwix was equally certain of his inability to give the inspector an idea what the unusual signature was intended to convey.

"Why didn't Kent pass the letter on to me? Why keep it a secret?"

"We gathered—that is I—" Myron floundered uncertainly, then plunged desperately straight ahead. "In fact Kent stated that he felt the police had made no progress toward solving the mystery surrounding his father's death, and suggested that we three try our hand at discovering where this threatening letter came from and what it meant. He believed it connected with the one that so upset his father on the last day of his life."

"He wanted you three to start playing detectives on your own hook?"

"Yes.

"Made any move in the suggested direction?

"No. We couldn't decide where to begin."

"Just as well, you'd probably have clogged up the works. Listen, is that your front door bell ringing?"

"It's the house-'phone—somebody downstairs.

"Why does no one answer it?"

"I expect the maids are all in bed, sir, they knew it was my night on duty," Fargo quietly explained.

"Then you'd better see if that's the men from headquarters. Suppose you go with him, Mr. Stanwix?"

The inspector was evidently unwilling to let any of the group out of his sight, alone, so delegated the office of playing eyes for him to Mark Stanwix. They came back after a reasonable interval followed by the medical examiner, several of Fisk's plainclothes men, and two electricians. He rapidly explained to the latter what was wanted, told Fargo to show them the penthouse fuse box and whatever else they needed to see, then whispered a few directions to Quinn, one of his operatives, who nodded understandingly and followed butler and electricians from the room.

The newcomers had brought flashlights and with the help of one held by his assistant, the doctor commenced a cursory examination of Kent Cardigan's body, while Inspector Fisk gave his men a hurried outline of events leading up to, and immediately following the murder.

He had taken them to the end of the room farthest from the men grouped near the mantelpiece so that while the latter remained in full view, they were unable to overhear his low-toned directions to his own men.

"They haven't been searched yet," Fisk finished, eyes intently watching for any betraying sign or movement among the suspects, "but they shall be, unless we find the knife elsewhere, for one of them must be guilty. It would have been comparatively easy for whoever killed young Cardigan to afterwards throw the knife out through a window before Fargo brought in a lamp, but if that was done it must still be there on the roof; that is, unless it went over the edge and I think the distance too great for that to be possible. Search the roof carefully, not only for the death-weapon but for signs of an intruder; there must have been an accomplice either there, or inside the house for those lights never went out of their own accord just at the critical instant."

"And the key, sir, that you say young Cardigan had in his hand when the lights were put out?" Clancy, one of his most intelligent younger operatives, eagerly inquired.

"Nothing seen of it so far, but of course the room hasn't been searched as I was alone and hadn't even a decent light. Kent may have dropped it when he was struck, or the murderer may have tried to take it from him and killed Kent when he refused to give it up."

"Was there a struggle?"

"Not that anybody heard. The room was full of muffled, confused sounds and that damned clock kept clanging the hour. Now, spread out over the roof, I'll carry on here alone until the lamps are fixed, then you'd better come back, Clancy, and help me look for the key we can't let anyone who was in the room out of our sight until it, and the knife, are found."

When they had gone Fisk watched until he could see them quartering the flagged terrace outside the windows, the prying rays of their torches playing over sunken flower beds and potted shrubs, then turned back to his interrupted questioning.

"I think you gentlemen have told all you can, or will, of what happened while the room was dark. Now perhaps the ladies won't mind saying where they were, and what doing, immediately before they came in here."

"If you think I can tell you anything, anything at all, while Kent's body stays there under our eyes you're utterly mistaken!" Faith lifted a tear-streaked face to indignantly stare at him. "While he's there I can't even *think* about anything else. Please, please do something—"

Realizing that the vehement protest was natural enough as coming from the lips of an inexperienced girl, Fisk consulted the medical examiner and finding him now quite ready to have the body moved to another room where it could be more thoroughly examined, told Faith to again cover her eyes.

When the big, limp frame so lately full of abounding, joyous life had been carried out, Faith consented to answering whatever questions the inspector chose to ask.

"From what Fargo said, I suppose all the bungalow lights went out, not simply those in the hall and this room," he began. "Where were you at the time?"

"In the music room."

"Miss Fane was with you?"

"No, I was quite alone."

"For how long?"

"From the time Mr. Page came in to tell us you and father wanted to talk with Kent; he, and Murray and my brother all left the music room with Mr. Page."

"Where was Miss Fane?"

"Why, I'm sure I don't know. She had gone out on the terrace a little while before that."

"Yet you and she came in here together."

"Because we ran into one another in the hall—"

"From what direction did she come?"

"I don't know. I didn't think about it."

"You can't say if she was headed toward, or away, from this room?"

"I haven't the faintest idea. Daphne whispered to me before I knew she was there—I was only too glad to find someone, the sudden darkness had frightened me."

"Did anyone else pass you in the hall?"

"I think not, though of course I can't be sure."

"And you, Miss Fane?" He turned to look directly into her wide open, amber-gold eyes. "Where were you when the lights went out?"

"A few feet from the terrace door. I had just come inside and had taken perhaps a half dozen steps when the hall became suddenly dark. I stood perfectly still expecting the lights to go on again, when they didn't I moved forward, cautiously, and presently heard a soft rustle and a little catching of the breath that I recognized as a habit of Faith's. I whispered her name so as not to startle her, and just then we could both see a reflected light shining out through the study door—of course the sound of your moving about and of some brief exclamations became audible the instant that door was opened."

"Ah!" Fisk leaned nearer. "Then the study door was closed at first? You heard nothing that went on in here until somebody opened it?"

"Of course I didn't think about it at the time, but yes, the door must have been shut at first."

"Fargo opened it?"

"How should I know? It was much too dark to see."

"You're not sure if anyone was in the hall besides yourself and Miss Stanwix?"

"I've no opinion either way."

"But—" he hesitated the fraction of a second—"but earlier in the evening you all knew there was to be a conference in the study tonight?"

"The others may have done, I personally knew nothing about it. Aren't you inclined to forget, inspector, that I'm a comparative stranger here? Faith's the only one I know at all well."

"Please let me say we none of us regard you as a stranger." It was Myron Stanwix who spoke. Unperceived by Fisk he had edged so close that he was almost touching the latter's elbow.

"I think you were asked to stay with the other men until the lights come on and we have a chance to search this room." He eyed the son of the house with open disapproval. "The gravity of the situation doesn't seem to have penetrated at all; yet to the average intelligence it's evident enough that one or other of you is about to be accused of murder."

"Nonsense, inspector! You can't seriously believe that any of us would kill Kent!"

"No? Perhaps you find it easier to believe that some disembodied spirit, and one capable of handling a knife at that, floated in, committed the murder, then gently melted away into thin air? Personally I find a human agency easier to credit." He paused to let his words sink in.

"When six men are grouped in a room suddenly plunged into three or four minutes' darkness, and at the end of that time one of their number is discovered dead—it's safe to conclude that one of the remaining five struck the fatal blow. I'm damn sure I didn't; remains, Whitney Page, Murray Sanger, your father and yourself."

As if to prove the often stated folly of completely unqualified assertion of any fact, the inspector's man, Clancy, here suddenly bobbed into view just outside one of the opposite windows and excitedly beckoned his chief.

"The knife?" Fisk crossed the room at a rapid lope and shot the question before Clancy had time to speak.

"We haven't found it, but there's a rope ladder dangling over the edge of the roof and a long silk cord flung down,

anyhow, near one of the flower beds. Come and look for
yourself, chief, there're marks in the earth of the same
flower bed that look as if somebody'd cleaned a knife there
inside of an hour at most."

11

ORANGE-YELLOW TULIPS

"You believe Kent Cardigan was killed by a knife thrown in through the open window, not by a blow struck by somebody already in the room with him?"

The inspector nodded, indulged in a long pull at the whiskey and soda thoughtfully provided by the Stanwix' attentive butler, then asked:

"Don't you agree?"

"I suppose so, though I've not yet sufficiently mastered the facts to form a decided opinion."

Sydney Traherne had arrived on the scene some time previously but there had been so much to do that it was only now, when the east was beginning to faintly lighten, that the two friends found themselves alone in the otherwise deserted study.

"At first I naturally took it for granted that one of the four men in the room with us had killed Kent—with the just possible inclusion of Fargo in my circle of suspects as there was no telling at exactly what instant he came in from the hall. There seemed a chance that he'd entered as soon as the lights went out and if so he could have committed the murder and thrown the weapon outside before he openly announced that he'd brought a lamp."

"You think the outside evidence clears him, as well as the others?"

"Hanged if I dare say for certain. There's something fishy about the man. Though he plays the part to perfection I'll bet he's no more an authentic butler than I am."

"There I'm with you," Traherne agreed. "All the signs point to Fargo's being close to the heart of this mystery."

"You don't think him the actual murderer, do you?"

"As I said before—my ideas are still fluid, they haven't settled into definite shape."

"Well, as things look now he can't be guilty," Fisk decided after a pause in which he mentally checked over impressions and time. "He couldn't have killed Kent, cleaned the knife in that flower bed, and still showed up with the lamp when he did. The bed's too far away from these windows and from the door leading in from the terrace—he couldn't possibly have made it in the time. Queer thing, have you noticed? here's the second murder where we've the precise instant at which it was committed all nicely checked up for us."

"First the bank clock showing what time the parade passed it, and now the one here striking midnight." Traherne nodded, but offered no comment on the rather curious coincidence. "Is the flower bed close to where your men found the rope ladder?"

"Yes, between it and the window near which Kent was standing. And by the way, it's not made of ordinary rope but of thick silk cord, similar, only heavier, to that with which Peter Cardigan was strangled."

"So? And the one flung down by the flower bed?"

"That's a twin to the one left in Mr. Cardigan's office. Did I tell you after the lights were repaired and we could see more distinctly I found a few loose frazzles of silk caught in a shutter catch of that window sill?"

He indicated the one he meant and Traherne's noncommittal eyes studied it thoughtfully.

"How far away from it was Kent standing?"

"Four or five feet perhaps. Why?"

"Only wondering how the murderer could aim so accurately in the dark."

"He or she, must have been crouching just outside the window and located his exact position while the lights were still burning."

"Did I imagine a faint emphasis on that 'she'?"

The inspector ran perplexed fingers through his already tousled hair. "If you did it was because I had Daphne Fane in mind. That woman's got me completely puzzled. First, we know she was here last night when we made plans for this midnight conference, presumably asleep—but was she? And now—I don't know if I told you that she complained of headache and went out on the terrace some little time before Whitney Page went to the music room for Kent Cardigan. Of course there's a good expanse of the main building's roof surrounding this penthouse on all four sides, still if she was innocently roaming about out there, alone, isn't it peculiar that she saw or heard nothing of the murderer's activities?"

"He'd aim for quietness, you know," Traherne interrupted with a half smile. "There'd be no unnecessary noise about his ascent of that ladder; or is it your idea that he used the thing only for a quick escape and not as a means of entry?"

"Hard to say. It was fixed to the roof edge by two steel hooks and the lower end dangled just in front of a hall window of the main building's top floor. I don't know if it would be possible to throw the ladder up from below in such a way that the hooks would catch on the parapet and hold."

"It's often been done when nothing more dangerous than a high wall had to be climbed," Traherne pointed out, "and the fact that he'd be working at such a perilous height wouldn't deter our man; his exploit in walking that ledge to enter Peter Cardigan's study proves a little thing like twenty-two or three stories means nothing to him."

"Must be a human spider," the inspector's tone sounded abused. "But the ladder's presence does seem to let Daphne Fane out. She not only couldn't use it, there'd be no earthly reason why she should want to. Though mind you—" he added on a distinctly belligerent note, "I still don't trust her. Her turning up here, almost a complete stranger, on the very day Peter Cardigan's murder was discovered was a bit too opportune, to say nothing of the way she's sticking when an ordinary guest would naturally make some excuse for going away. I believe she knows a lot more than she's told about the entire mystery."

"Have you tried to learn who she is and where Faith Stanwix met her?"

"Yes, I've a man working that angle but so far he only reports her as a member of the Greenwich house party; a fact we already knew. Faith seems to have met her there for the first time, and as Daphne's supposed to be a stranger in New York, invited her to stop here until she sailed for Europe."

"But she must have come from somewhere to join this house party."

"Quite so, only my man can't discover where. She simply turned up one morning in her own car, loaded with luggage, and was cordially received and welcomed by the master of the house."

"License plate?"

"A brand new one labeled Detroit, Michigan."

"Terribly helpful," Traherne sympathized.

"Yes, isn't it? And speaking of cars, you've not had time to tell me about the smash up in which Cardigan's salesman was killed."

"It wasn't precisely a smash up," Traherne quietly corrected, "or at least only in the sense that Roberts himself

was very effectually smashed. It happened on a side road
where there's very little traffic and there were no witnesses
except a couple of small boys who say he was taking a
short cut leading to an outlying station, when a long gray
car deliberately ran him down and rushed on its way; they
hadn't time, or presence of mind, to get its license number."

"If the incident was as simple as that, what the devil
kept you so long?"

"I spent a goodish bit of time trying to trace Roberts'
movements in New Haven before the accident, as it's officially called. He'd put up at a rooming house, not a hotel,
and late last night, or rather Monday night, one of his fellow roomers met him down by the railroad tracks running
along the shore. I'm wondering if he went there to dispose
of the briefcase he carried when last seen in Troy? It wasn't
near his body, or in the room he'd engaged for only one
night."

"Humph, even at that I don't see why you were so late
getting here. Over the 'phone you said you meant starting
back directly after dinner."

"Engine trouble."

"Oh! No garage on the post road, I suppose."

"Sarcasm quite unwarranted. I'm telling you the actual
truth—only, well you see it wasn't ordinary engine trouble. Putting it plainly, I think I wasn't meant to reach New
York tonight."

"Suffering cats! You mean your car was tampered with?"

"Well, does it seem reasonable that an engine running
smooth as silk on the outward trip should develop half a
dozen different ailments in widely separated sections of its
anatomy, while it quietly waited in a New Haven garage?"

"But how could it be got at in a public garage?

"I imagine a remark dropped by the garage owner—
which passed over my head at the time of its utterance—

gives a clue. When I collected the car and paid its fee he said he hoped I'd have no more engine trouble. Probably someone dressed as a mechanic claimed I'd sent him to make repairs, and tinkered with the engine right under the garage owner's unsuspicious nose."

"Sid, this is getting serious. They might have decided to put you out of commission instead of your car."

"Quite. But apparently delay was all they aimed at, not permanent removal. And by the way, I notice we've both suddenly taken to the plural."

"Necessary. Kent's murder couldn't have been a one-man job, the lights prove that, for the electricians from headquarters say the entire current was cut off by someone who knew his business, and it's obvious he'd orders to sever the connection at precisely twelve o'clock; our murderer couldn't have been in two places at once."

"And the motive. Think Kent Cardigan was killed for sake of his father's safe deposit key?"

"Only to prevent his using it, apparently, since we found the key itself when the lights were repaired."

"Where?"

Inspector Fisk reluctantly dragged his tired body from the comfortable depths of his chair and went across to show the exact spot; Traherne following close at his heels.

"Here, close to the leg of that desk. It showed plainly enough once the lights came on again."

"And Kent Cardigan—where was he standing?"

"About here." Fisk moved several feet closer to the window, assuming, as nearly as he could remember it, the position of the murdered man when the room went dark.

"So?" his friend reflectively eyed the distance between the two spots. "Knowing its importance, one would rather expect Kent's hand to clutch the key when he was struck, instead of throwing it so faraway."

"Perhaps his idea was to keep the murderer from getting it."

"He had time to think, then? He didn't die instantly?"

"It must have been a good two minutes, or even a trifle longer, between his scream and the time we got the lamp decently lighted. We all saw his final death spasm. Though of course I can't say if he lost consciousness the instant he was stabbed. He uttered no cry."

Very thoughtfully, Traherne returned to his former seat, remaining silent while he replenished his glass and slowly sampled its contents.

"The motive seems to hinge on that key and the deposit box to which it gives access," he finally meditated aloud. "Question. Does it hold some thing of immense value, or some secret that would ruin the murderer if it once came to light? Well, we ought to be able to answer tomorrow, for now Kent's dead I suppose Mark Stanwix will hardly object to opening the box himself in his capacity as the principal executor of old Peter Cardigan's will."

"The subject wasn't brought up tonight but he's unlikely to make any difficulty. In fact, considering what happened to Kent when they'd no reason to be sure he meant ignoring their warning, I should think Stanwix would be glad to get rid of all responsibility."

"Warning? What warning?" Traherne abruptly abandoning his easily lounging poise, caught sharply at the one word.

"Why, I told you Kent got a warning letter in this morning's, or rather yesterday morning's mail."

"You told me nothing of the kind, this is the first I've heard of any letter. Did Kent pass it on to you?"

"No, he kept mum as an oyster. It wasn't till after he was dead that young Stanwix told me, and when the medical examiner and I searched Kent's pockets we found the letter carefully tucked away." Fisk dug into an inner pocket, producing a large bill-fold from which he fished out a single sheet of heavy note paper. "Here it is."

Traherne took it gingerly. "Been gone over for finger prints, of course?"

"Naturally, but whoever wrote it used gloves; we found only the prints of the three inseparables, who'd all read it, and our own."

Traherne opened it out and thoughtfully studied the line or two of curiously thick characters.

"WHEN KEY IS DELIVERED TOSS FROM STUDY WINDOW WITHOUT USING."

"So? It's lined with a fine camel's-hair brush, not written with a pen," he mused. "Much more difficult to link with anybody's normal handwriting, of course, as the technique of the two methods differs so widely. What do you make of the little drawing in place of a signature?"

"It's crudely done—might be meant to represent a black cat."

"Or a Panther."

"What!" Fisk's heels, which had been restfully cocked on a table edge, came to the floor with a resounding bang. "A panther?"

"Quite so—panther—panther's den—our night club seems to be coming closer into the picture and, incidentally, I think we can now hazard a guess about that missing drawing which so terrified Peter Cardigan when it reached him at luncheon time on Saturday."

"Nonsense, man! You're letting your penchant for that night club carry you off at an absurd tangent."

"Think so?" Traherne's eyes were narrowed to mere slits, into which the gradually strengthening daylight struck with an oddly glittering effect.

"I do. What possible connection could there be between a club of that type—questionable, to say the least of it—and a wealthy, conservative old family like the Cardigans?"

"Conservative, and wealthy families *have* been known to possess something for which clever members of the underworld decidedly hankered," Traherne pointed out. "Taken separately the incidents pointing to a hidden connection between the Cardigan family and the Panther's Den don't carry much weight, but once added together they gain tremendously in cumulative value.

"First, that new black and white vanity case found in Peter Cardigan's room, an expensive toy presumably intended as a present for someone who favored that particular color scheme.

"Second, Kent's presence in the night club so soon after his father's murder and his quite evident absorption in the girl of the jungle dance, a strictly black and white specialty if you'll remember.

"Third, the Stanwix butler's visit to the Panther's Den and his mysterious disappearance, a disappearance as my own expedition proved, that actually meant his entry into the more private and secret depths of the Panther's Den.

"And now we've this anonymous letter signed with a sketch that I believe is most certainly meant to represent that animal, and on top of it all, Kent's murder the instant after his receipt of the safety deposit key. Can you honestly dismiss that list with the hackneyed explanation 'coincidence'?"

"But—" The inspector hesitated, struggling to read his friend's lean, inscrutable face. "You seem to be hinting at something closer, more intimate, than a crook, or gang of crooks' desire to rob Peter Cardigan."

"Unless I'm all wrong there's a personal element in this case. For one thing this mysterious Panther is too well informed—he seems to know every move here before it's actually made. Question. Does Fargo's presence in the bungalow fully account for that?"

"Tell me more details about your visit to the night club," Fisk demanded, his interest now thoroughly aroused. "Yesterday you sketched what happened, but the news of Roberts' death came before you'd finished and you dashed off to New Haven, dropping me where the jungle girl took you into her dressing room."

"Nearly enough the end of the story. There was no more excitement after that. She simply hid me behind some costumes hanging in her closet and when the gang who were after me came to the door vowed she'd seen nothing of any stranger. After they'd gone she dosed me with an unholy mixture of clambroth and spirits of ammonia to sober me up. Later, when the pursuit had died a natural death, she sneaked me out by way of a back exit; warning me never to show my nose in any part of that building again. Then she smiled at me—she's a sweet, wide-eyed sort of grin, something like a small kid's—and told me it wasn't safe to take an interest in the Panther's Cub; a title of which she appeared inordinately proud."

"What is she to him, the Panther, I mean? And did you gather his exact position in the club?"

"The girls I sat with while watching the telephone booths dropped a few hints. I gather he owns the club, the whole building in fact, but never puts in a personal appearance. Both girls claimed that while they'd been employed there for upward of a year, they'd neither of them ever seen the Panther."

"And the black and white girl who rescued you?"

"One said she's his daughter, the other his mistress. I doubt if they were doing more than repeat the current gossip of the club. They grew quite heated over the question of the Panther's age, the one who upheld the daughter theory claiming he was an elderly man, the other that he was young, must be, because twice since she'd been working there he had unexpectedly taken the place of Mitza's ordinary partner, or partners, and danced a variation of whatever specialty number she happened to be doing at the time."

"But I thought you just now said neither of them had ever seen him?"

"They meant to get any idea of his actual identity. They both saw him dance with the Panther's Cub, but in costumes that didn't reveal his face. In fact the father-theory girl declared it wasn't the Panther who danced at all, but someone representing him to throw people off the trail of what he was really like."

"Queer mix up, any way you look at it. I'm beginning to take a keen interest in this mysterious Panther." Fisk considered what Traherne had just told him and its possible bearing on the Cardigan case. "Why not raid the place, say tonight, and see what we can discover?"

"It would be precious little," Traherne predicted. "Remember the Panther owns the entire building, or so I gathered from those girls and from my own experience, even if you threw a cordon around the whole block the place is a veritable rabbit's-warren of small rooms and passages that it would take a small army to explore. You might find where they keep their cellar, but not much else, and it's a moral certainty that the Panther doesn't live there himself, though by the comfortable way the top floor is furnished I imagine some of his people do."

"You mean we'd get no idea of his main racket? What do you suppose it is, by the way? Any theories?"

"Hard to say, definitely—but the scene where the whispering voice spoke through the grill pretty well shows he's other activities outside the night club itself. A man who is as careful as that not to let his own followers see him, or hear his real voice, would never be fool enough to let himself be trapped in a police raid. No, we'll discover more if I go back alone."

"You're idiot enough to risk going back, after once getting away with a whole skin?"

"Oh, the risk's not so great. Nobody got a clear look at me after I'd negotiated that trick 'phone booth and I doubt if anyone noticed me especially in the supper room itself. Even if they did the strongest reason for connecting that particular patron with the intruder who afterwards stirred up trouble in the club's inner regions, would be the fact that I left without settling my bill; and I think my reappearance and explanation that I simply forgot, will partially discount that. They won't expect such brazen procedure, not if I was really spying, that is."

"This jungle girl will recognize you."

"Mitza? Yes, I want her to. She's my best hope of gaining information. She fully believed I was drunk and simply hunting for her, and won't give me away."

"Frankly, Sid, I don't like it. This Panther seems to have no earthly compunction about snuffing out a life that gets in his way."

"Admitted, providing he's actually responsible for all these murders; a fact of which we haven't an iota of proof."

"Sounds a bit like craw-fishing, that." The inspector's glance was a puzzled interrogation mark. "First you're hot on the Panther's trail, next you seem to suggest that the blood-guilt may not lie at his door. Strikes me, Sid, that you're not being altogether frank over this case."

"Give you my word that I'm not holding out on you, if that's what you mean. You're possessed of every fact I am, and if I happen to have drawn certain inferences from them that slightly differ from yours, as yet they're much too vague for putting into words."

As he spoke Traherne had been absently staring at an earthen pot filled with tulip plants in gaudy blossom, now, as the gradually strengthening daylight brought out their vivid orange-yellow, he leant forward to softly stroke one of the flowers with a caressing finger-tip.

"Pretty, aren't they?"

The inconsequential remark drew a contemptuous snort from Conway Fisk, but it also served to call his attention to the fact that day had now fairly broken. He got a little stiffly to his feet; it had been a long, exhausting night.

"Come outside and have a look at the rope ladder and disturbed flower bed by daylight. This room faces west and we can search it more effectually when the light's a bit stronger."

"Right." Traherne crushed out his cigarette and stood up, still eyeing the tulips. "Only put one of your men on duty here while we're gone; we can't risk having a stray housemaid disturbing anything."

12

Two Flakes of Wax

None of the penthouse inmates had been phlegmatic enough to obtain more than broken snatches of sleep so that they began drifting into the dining room in quest of breakfast, at a most unconscionably early hour. Fargo, as immaculately correct as if no tragedy had occurred during the past night, served first his young master, then Faith, and lastly Daphne Fane, Mr. Stanwix himself having sent word that he preferred breakfasting in his own room.

All three were silent, almost constrained, as Fargo supplied them with coffee and offered food which none of them did much more than make a pretense of eating. Faith's eyes were faintly reddened as if she had been crying and her brother's dark face looked oddly shadowed, almost sunken, at cheeks and temples, only Daphne Fane's clear-skinned beauty remained unflawed in the harsh morning light.

"Faith—" it was Daphne who finally broke the strained silence. "Faith says I'm wrong in thinking that under the circumstances I ought to go away. But surely after what's happened you must all feel a house-guest rather a burden."

"We don't!" Faith hurriedly denied, though it was Myron whom her friend had directly addressed. "Having you with us is a very great comfort—and surely if there was ever a time when I needed a friend, it's now."

Still Daphne waited, her eyes on Myron, and it was only when he very cordially seconded his sister's refusal to let her leave them that Daphne yielded the point with a warmly grateful smile.

"It's dear of you both to want me, but—if I'm really to stay you must let me help."

"Help? How do you mean?" There was a sudden note of anxiety in Myron's voice.

"It's like this—" She abandoned all pretense of eating and pushing her plate aside lighted a cigarette. "Mr. Cardigan was killed last Saturday and this is Wednesday—the police don't seem to have discovered a solitary clue as to who did it, or why. And now they've let poor Kent share his father's fate practically under Inspector Fisk's very nose. Don't you honestly think it's about time something was done about it?"

"Who told you that Kent expressed the same opinion yesterday afternoon, and that we three 'Inseparables' planned taking a hand ourselves?" Myron sharply demanded.

"Nobody. In fact I didn't know it. I just thought about it all, last night when I couldn't sleep, and decided the police were proving frightfully incompetent."

"She's perfectly right," Faith eagerly agreed. "We three, and Murray of course, ought to try and discover the truth. If we let the inspector and his friend just go on puttering about, not accomplishing a thing, goodness knows *who* may be murdered next!"

"But we none of us have the haziest idea how detectives work," her brother objected. "How on earth could we hope to discover anything?"

"I don't know, but at least it's better to try than to sit around with our hands folded, waiting for somebody else to be killed." She stopped short almost on a gasp, her dark eyes widening as she struggled to capture and coordinate some new thought that had flashed into her mind. "Wait—let me think a second. I believe Kent told me something that may give us a clue the inspector knows nothing about."

"What sort of clue?" Daphne caught at her hand, while Myron watched them a grayish pallor slowly over-spreading his face.

"You know, Daphne, both Kent Cardigan and Murray Sanger have always been almost like two extra brothers to me. Our fathers were all close friends and we children grew up together; the bond between us knit closer, perhaps, because all our mothers died when we were fairly small; Murray's when he was only a baby. Well, knowing each other so intimately, they both confided in me as much, if not more, than Myron did, and about two months ago, just when Murray and I were beginning to think we cared for each other, Kent told me he'd fallen in love!"

"Not really?" Myron's tone expressed the liveliest amazement. "He never said a word to me—he was always girl-shy."

"Maybe he told me because he thought I'd sympathize on account of falling in love myself."

"Don't you think, if we mean trying to solve this mystery, just by our own efforts, that we ought to send for Mr. Sanger and let him hear what Kent told Faith?"

"Yes, yes, of course we ought!" Myron jumped up, his manner suddenly as eagerly interested as his sister's. "I'll go 'phone him!"

While he was gone Fargo, who had discreetly slipped from the room when the conversation took a personal turn, came back with a fresh pot of coffee, then disappeared again as Myron reentered.

"He couldn't sleep any more than the rest of us, and says he'll be up in half a jiffy."

When Murray Sanger had joined them Faith proceeded to tell them exactly what Kent had confided to her.

"He told me he'd fallen in love, desperately, with a girl whom he'd met when some friends took him to a night club where she worked as a dancer. He was plain crazy about her, and terribly unhappy because he believed she was too young and innocent to realize the danger of working in a place like that, and also because she wouldn't let him really talk to her or tell her how much he cared.

"You both must know," she glanced from her brother to Murray Sanger, "how queerly trusting Kent was when he deeply liked a person. He never seemed able to see their faults, or to believe them anything less than perfect, but— please don't think me horridly evil-minded—what he told me about this girl and the way she'd half led him on, half evaded him, didn't sound as if she was really the innocent little victim of a hard necessity to earn her living that he believed. Perhaps I hurt Kent by letting him see that I didn't altogether sympathize, for he never mentioned her again and I'd almost forgotten until just now, when it occurred to me that his infatuation for this dancer may be in some way connected with his death. Couldn't he, perhaps, have made enemies by trying to take her away from the club where she worked? One reads and hears of such things happening."

"At least Kent's loving the girl, and visiting this night club secretly, that is without telling Murray or me, gives us a sort of lead which I think we ought to follow," Myron declared.

"But his father—Kent's having roused the jealousy, or enmity of the dancer's associates couldn't account for his father's murder," Daphne objected.

"How can we be sure?" From having at first blown cold on the scheme of personal investigation into the mystery surrounding the two Cardigan murders, Myron had switched to the plan's most enthusiastic advocate. "Let's all four of us visit the club tonight. What's its name, Faith, and where is it?"

"Why—" his sister stared at him with a certain blank dismay, "I'm afraid I've forgotten—you see it was two months ago!"

"That's an encouraging sample of how far we're likely to go running a private inquiry on our own." Sanger lighted a cigarette, smiling indulgently at Faith's still dismayed expression. "Won't it be wiser to tell the inspector of Kent's incipient love affair and throw in our forces with his?"

"No," she mutinously refused. "He wouldn't tell us anything, or let us try to help. Besides if I think hard enough I'm sure the name will come back to me. I know it had something to do with an animal."

"Shall I cut across to the library and fetch some books on Zoology?" Sanger offered, an amused flicker in the gray eyes he tried to make as serious as the others.

"Don't be stupid!" for once Faith's voice lost the tender note it habitually held when she spoke to him. "Den. The name had a den in it. A lion's or a tiger's—no—that's not right! Oh, dear, why can't I remember?"

"It wasn't by any chance the Panther's Den, was it?" Daphne inquired.

"Yes, oh yes, that's it! How in the world did you know? Surely Kent didn't tell you about it?"

"Of course not, why I scarcely knew him. It simply happens that a friend of mine told me about a club of that name when he heard I was to spend a week or two in New York. He advised a visit and even gave me the address. I'm nearly sure it's still in my writing case, I'll go and get it."

She was gone barely ten minutes but when she returned Murray Sanger was alone, standing near but slightly back from, one of the windows overlooking the terrace.

"Their father sent for them," he replied to her question as to what had become of Faith and Myron.

Daphne hesitated a second, then very softly closed the door through which she had just entered and crossing the room stood looking out past his shoulder to where Inspector Fisk, Sydney Traherne, and a uniformed officer could be seen talking together.

"Do you suppose they've discovered anything?"

"Probably not, the police seldom do. I saw some of the inspector's men quartering the roof when I arrived by way of the stairs and they didn't look at all pleased with themselves."

"It's odd, how you all live and have your offices in this same building."

"But I, for one, haven't," he absently assured her, still watching the three earnestly talking men outside. "My apartment's on the 20th floor but I don't boast an office either here, or anywhere else."

"No? Please don't tell me you're an artist, or a writer or anything like that. It wouldn't at all fit my conception of you, you seem such an out-of-door type of person."

"Do I? Well, perhaps I am a bit over-fond of sports, and dad worked so hard and so wisely, that there's no wolf at the door insisting that I should work."

"Oh!" Both her hands suddenly clutched his arm, drawing him further away from the window. "The inspector's turning this way! Don't let him see us."

"Why not?" Sanger's cool gray eyes studied the fingers that looked so delicately white against the dark cloth of his coat sleeve. "Surely we've no reason to hide. Unless you're already suffering from a guilty conscience because we intend holding back information from the police."

"I haven't that kind of a conscience." Her fingers stirred softly but showed no inclination to withdraw from his rigidly unresponsive arm.

"No?" Sanger's pointed eyebrows climbed an amused fraction of an inch. "Of what kind then? I'm willing to bet it's of a strictly feminine variety."

"That sounds a trifle disparaging. Don't you think we have as keen a sense of honor as you men?"

"But certainly—only its cutting edge deals more in personal, less in universal codes. Most women find little difficulty in making themselves believe the most elaborately curved course of action straight as a string, if only it works to the advantage of someone they love."

"Whereas when you men swerve from the prescribed straightness it's usually for some purely selfish reason," she retorted with the softest whisper of a laugh. "Look! I think they're coming this way." This last with reference to Sydney Traherne and the inspector.

"Well, so far we've done nothing that needs to be hidden."

"No, but I'm sure we look like a couple of conspirators, peering out like this."

In spite of her declared anxiety not to be seen, she leaned closer to him in the effort to see where the two men on the terrace were going, so that Sanger could feel the firm curve of her breast pressing against his arm. Was it a deliberate gesture, he wondered, or had her interest made her oblivious of how close they stood? The little imp of mischievous curiosity never long dormant in his mind, prompted him to gently stir the arm against which she leaned.

Her instant response reminded him of the movement with which an affectionate feline rubs against a caressing hand and those quizzical eyebrows of his climbed a fraction higher, while an irresistible chuckle whispered in the depths of his throat. Then, with a quite unmistakable finality, he freed his arm and went back to the breakfast table, helping himself to a cup of the now tepid coffee. They were standing with the width of the table between them when Myron and Faith came back.

After Inspector Fisk had reentered the penthouse Sydney Traherne continued to prowl around the roof, pursuing some private and unspecified investigation of his own.

One matter into which he very thoroughly inquired was the number, and location, of the various entrances and exits; they were five in all, with only two of them in general use. Besides the elevator that brought passengers up from the lower floors of the building, and the stairway running down to the main block of apartments, the two modes of entrance in constant use, there was the strictly private elevator connecting the Stanwix penthouse with the bank of which its owner was president and two enclosed circular staircases designed for escape in case of fire; both of these latter kept always locked though every tenant in the building possessed a key.

Having learned all he could about stairways and elevators, Traherne took one last look at the rope ladder still dangling from the roof edge, then joined Conway Fisk in the study.

"Are Peter Cardigan's papers and account books still in his office, or have they been taken down to headquarters?" he presently inquired, while they both inspected the room and its furnishings more thoroughly than had been possible by artificial light.

"They've been pretty carefully gone over," his friend responded, "but there seems nothing wrong with them, so they're still in the office. Why?"

"Just wanted a leisurely look with no one to hurry me."

"Go ahead and have it, now, if you like. I'll join you when I've finished here."

"Right."

But he did not go immediately, instead he went close to the desk and stooping, picked up two tiny flakes of a whitish substance that had caught and reflected the now strong daylight.

"You said nothing about using candles last night, when the lights were out."

"For the very good reason that we didn't use any. My electric torch refused to work and we'd nothing but the lamp Fargo brought in, until the electricians had repaired the damage."

"That's singular." Traherne extended his open palm, "I just found two flakes of wax on the rug near that desk leg."

"Most likely dropped when the housemaid last polished the furniture, or the floor." Fisk was paying what he said only a divided attention. "Come over here and take another look at these windows. Do you agree that they're too high from the ground for anyone to have climbed in and out last night?"

"Not only that, the soft loam of the flower bed running under all three windows is innocent of foot prints. I examined it myself after you came inside."

"So Clancy reported. But as you doubtless noticed, the bed stops flush with the side of this window close to which Kent Cardigan stood. It's my idea that the killer kept close against the house with his feet on the flagging that starts just there, and avoided stepping on the soft earth. Standing like that the curtains would shield him from the sight of anyone inside the room, while the light was burning, whereas he'd be able to see through, or around them enough to take aim at Kent's white shirt front."

"Quite." Traherne strolled to the table holding the potted tulips, stood for a second admiring their fiery blossoms, then calmly collected the pot in the crook of one arm and started for the door. "Under the circumstances I'm sure nobody'll object if I walk off with these. I always did think yellow such a psychic color."

13

A Gaudy Handkerchief

"I thought you said Peter Cardigan's firm only sold stocks and bonds?" Traherne laid down a sheaf of papers and turned to stare reproachfully at Inspector Fisk, who had just entered Peter Cardigan's private office.

"So I did." The inspector dropped wearily into a chair beside the desk at which his friend was working. "What's wrong with the statement?"

"First time I ever heard of importing those particular commodities."

"Are you by any chance trying to be funny?" Fisk cocked a tired but suspicious eye at Traherne's serious expression.

"Far from it—but if the firm dealt exclusively in negotiable paper, why so many entries charged to custom duties?"

"Oh that!" Fisk allowed himself the relaxation of a cigarette. "Our accountant noticed the number of import duties marked on the books and questioned Mr. Cardigan's stenographer. It seems he'd been abroad rather frequently and kept in touch with a good many dealers there; when they had some particularly good antiques to offer they let him know, and if any of his friends wanted them they were sent over in care of Mr. Cardigan."

"I see. Sort of supplementary dealing in curios outside his regular business."

"Not at all. The transactions were of a purely friendly nature, with nothing asked in the way of commission."

"No? Well to judge by the books he made up for that by charging his friends a stiffish duty on every article sent across. It's a wonder he didn't strike someone who knew the Government puts no duty on antiques over a hundred years old."

"For the love of Mike stop ranting about customs charges—they've not an earthly thing to do with this investigation—and let me spill my tale of woe," the inspector besought. "That old fool of a Mark Stanwix is suffering from what he calls conscientious scruples but I'd call it plain mulishness; he refuses to use that devilish key and open the safety deposit box around which all the trouble seems to center."

"Why?"

"Says Peter Cardigan left no instructions as to what should be done in case Kent died. Now they're both gone he feels uncertain how his old friend would like having strangers poking into his secrets."

"Rather suggests he knows more about the character of said secrets than he's so far admitted. Can't you force his hand by a Court order to open it in the interest of Justice?"

"Yes, but it will take a little time, what with this afternoon's inquest and all, I doubt if it can be managed today. Besides Stanwix may change his mind—I left Whitney Page trying to make him listen to reason. In the meantime we'd better lunch, if we mean having any before the inquest."

"I'm not attending it," Traherne calmly announced. "There won't be much more than the formal medical evidence and an adjournment. A few hours' solid sleep will be more to the point."

"Humph, I suppose such insistence on an afternoon nap means you still intend visiting the Panther's Den to-night?"

"Yes. And by the way, I'd like an operative—a clever one—to trail someone I'll point out if the little gods of chance favor our cause tonight."

"Prefer a man or a woman?"

"Better make it a woman, I think. Properly got up she'll attract less attention than a man. Send her to my apartment early this evening; I'll tell her what time to be at the club, and just what I want done."

"Right. And now for some lunch."

But the inspector's inner emptiness was not to be immediately comforted; Traherne called his attention to some queer little penciled marks running along the edge of the desk blotter.

"What do they look like to you?"

"Nothing in particular, except possibly a series of capital Cs, half of them facing the wrong way."

"Yes, either that or the outer rim of a human ear—but I've a feeling they're actually something quite different and I can't for the life of me put a name to it."

"Why do they matter?"

"I'm not at all sure that they do. But as you've probably noticed, a great many people when nervous, or thinking intently, scratch some sort of pattern on any convenient bit of paper—only it's nearly always the same design of loops, zig-zags, or scrolls. Since the process is purely automatic very few people ever vary the pattern, yet curiously enough in going over Peter Cardigan's papers I've run across several on which he's scratched another totally different design; this is the only one showing a string of capital Cs or ears. Rather indicates that they refer to something he had on his mind that last day of his life—for the stenographer tells me the blotter is a fresh one she herself put on the desk last Saturday morning."

"If the sketching is an automatic habit they probably mean nothing at all." Fisk eyed the wobbly little Cs, half of them facing in the opposite direction from the rest, with open disparagement.

"Doubtless you're right, all the same they worry me, I keep trying to think what they remind me of."

"No wonder it made Kent miserable to have the girl he loved dancing in a place like this!" Faith shivered and drew her chair a little closer to Murray Sanger's. "Only look at those men over there! Haven't they terribly criminal faces? And that woman! Painted and dressed like that at her age, it's horrible. She must be thoroughly bad!"

Which remark, could she have overheard it, would have been gratefully accepted by the woman in question as a tribute to her artistry in character make up, for she was the police operative furnished at Sydney Traherne's request by his friend the inspector.

"Try to ignore the sordid side," Daphne Fane advised. "Most of the people are of quite a different class, and there're some quite stunning men."

"Such as?" Sanger leaned toward her across the table. "I'm curious. Please point out one that exactly suits your taste."

"Shall I?" Her smile held a provocative element, faintly underlain by some more serious emotion which he found himself quite unable to decipher. "Well, I like men who are tall, slender, but beautifully built and dark—above all things dark! They must have sleepy looking brown eyes and smooth, thick black hair; the color scheme's even more important than the precise cut of the profile."

"Alas, my fond aspirations are not only cut down, they're trampled on!" Sanger laughed, wondering if she realized with what extreme precision she had described the Stanwix' handsome butler. "My coloring never was anything but nondescript—even the most doting admirer couldn't describe it as anything more vivid than a symphony of drabs and grays; while as for my profile, well, probably the less said the better."

"Ah! But your smile!" Heedless of Faith's sensitive shrinking from their casual banter, she laid a warm gloveless hand on the one that played with his silver. "That atones for any possible lack—it is the smile that's come down through the ages, charming women to their undoing, since the Great God Pan wore it in far off Greece."

"Flatterer! You'll have me sailing through life wearing a perpetual grin," he warned.

"Hush," Myron broke in almost rudely. "The orchestra is changing. Perhaps the next specialty is danced by the girl Kent—loved."

Brother and sister were at one in their dislike of the incipient flirtation that seemed to push them both into some chill outer region. If Daphne realized their disapproval she gave no sign, but Murray Sanger drained his glass with a quick, somewhat nervous gesture and thereafter devoted himself exclusively to Faith.

None of the four had noticed an interested observer occupying one of the recessed tables at some distance from their own. A man in a faintly rumpled dinner suit, with his hair unfashionably parted in the exact center of his head and unbecomingly plastered down against cheeks that were just a little reddened. One careful look would have revealed him to any of the four as Inspector Fisk's playwright friend who dabbled in crime detection, but none of the four bestowed that one observant glance and his presence in the Panther's Den remained quite unsuspected.

The next specialty was, in fact, the famous jungle dance of which Kent had told Faith enough to make her sure this small, exquisite black and white girl was the one he had loved. She watched the reality with a clearer understanding of what Kent had tried to express. The girl seemed so

young, so oddly innocent; perhaps it was that very quality
in her which robbed the sensuous dance of obtrusive sex-
uality.

When it was finished Murray Sanger scribbled a note of
invitation, submitted it for Myron's approval, then tipped
a waiter to hand it to the little dancer.

She had sat down, alone, at a small reserved table not
far from the arch leading to the telephone booths, and they
watched while she received and read the note, then asked
the waiter who had sent it. Moved by a sudden friendly
impulse Faith half rose as she saw the dancer looking in
their direction, but the girl's refusal to join them was instant and unmistakable. She shook her head in decisive
negative, blew a smiling kiss to Faith, then gave her whole
attention to the supper dishes on her own table.

"She almost never talks to anyone." Their waiter came
back to apologize for his non-success. "Just does her number, sometimes has a bite of supper and sometimes not,
then leaves the club and isn't seen again until next night."

"But I wrote we'd a special reason for asking her to
join us," Sanger complained. "We're friends of a friend of
hers."

"Begging your pardon, sir, that doesn't sound hardly
possible. I think you must have made some mistake. The
Panther's Cub isn't allowed to *have* any friends!"

Then, as if frightened by his own, burst of frankness,
the man turned and scuttled away; it was another waiter
who presently brought them their check and asked if there
was anything more they required.

Sydney Traherne had been an interested observer of the
whole little episode, and when it was over and the four
amateur detectives had taken a disappointed departure,
very little wiser than when they came, he sat on at his table
for some time. Had he better follow their example and
send Mitza a note or simply drift across and speak to her?

Deciding that the latter course held most hope, he paid for his supper and started for the main entrance—to change his course midway and swerve over to Mitza's table instead.

"Yes, I know you told me not to dare come back—but I couldn't keep away," he announced, calmly appropriating the vacant chair and meeting her startled eyes with a beaming smile.

"You—Oh, you unspeakable idiot! If you don't care about your own safety you might have decency enough to consider mine," she blazed at him, flags of scarlet rage in her cheeks showing even through their chalk-white make up.

"But I *had* to come back and make sure you hadn't suffered through helping me." He eyed her with the meek but slightly abused air of a dog that has been unjustly scolded.

"Oh, you're impossible—there was never such a fool before!" but her voice was kinder than the words it uttered.

"Call me a fool, call me anything you like, so long as you let me stay."

"Surely you sobered enough the other night to understand that I'm not allowed to have men friends."

"Then it's a cruel, outrageous crime, and whoever's responsible ought to be shot: making a prisoner of a beautiful girl like you!"

"Haven't you *any* brain at all? Can't you understand plain English?" She was half laughing, half exasperated. "I told you it's the man I love who doesn't want me to know other men—and I'm perfectly satisfied—if it wasn't for him and what he's taught me, I'd still be dancing in some rotten Brooklyn speakeasy instead of here."

"Maybe you'd be a lot freer there."

"But I don't want to be free, no woman does, not really—we're happiest doing exactly what the man we love wants us to."

"Tell me about it," he invited, leaning toward her across the disordered little table. "You see I've never been in love before, and there're so many things I'd like you to explain."

"If I only dared!" For a second she seemed gripped by the almost universal human craving to confide in some sympathetic listener, then some emotion, fear perhaps, or loyalty, checked the impulse. "No, it's not possible—unless—" She rose abruptly, staring at him out of big, haunted eyes. "Forget what I said before—come again tomorrow night and perhaps—I won't promise anything, but perhaps—"

She fled across the dancing floor and out through a little door beside the musician's platform. Leaving Traherne with a queer guilty feeling of not having played quite fair. In spite of her surroundings and her work, Mitza seemed almost like a child whom it wasn't altogether playing the game to deceive, no matter in how good a cause.

He was still rather guiltily weighing her words and manner as bearing on his own suspicions, when the sleek dark foreigner who, two nights ago, had received a tiny square of yellow silk from the unseen owner of the voice behind the grill, slipped quietly out from the trick phone booth and made for the club's main entrance.

Instantly quite another side of Traherne sprang into action. He stood up and producing a particularly gaudy handkerchief earnestly blew his nose, then waved the silk monstrosity in the foreigner's direction. It was the signal agreed upon; the woman with whose dress and make up Faith had found fault, quietly left the Panther's Den close at the unsuspecting Andre's heels.

14
Tibits

"Hark! What was that? I thought I heard someone moving on the terrace."

For a tense instant they all listened, glasses or cigarettes suspended in mid-air, then Murray Sanger regained his normal poise and emitted a derisive little snort.

"Got the jumps, all of us, that's what's wrong! Faith, my child, be good enough to stop hearing noises or you'll have us all hiding under the furniture."

"Just the same I *did* hear something," Faith quietly insisted.

"Nonsense," her brother spoke almost sharply, a most unusual thing with him. "That gruesome Panther's Den upset your nerves. I'm sorry we went."

"Might as well have stayed away for all the good it did us," Sanger agreed. "Methinks Faith's dancing-girl-clew has proved a distinct fizzle—the lady's much too exclusive."

"How *can* we get at her, do you suppose?" Daphne inquired of no one in particular. "Now that I've seen the girl I quite understand Kent Cardigan's getting all wrought up over her; a big blond man like that would be bound to go down in defeat before a black and white slip of a thing."

"Rather an expert in affairs of the heart—aren't you, Miss Fane?" There was the faintest edge of a sneer in Sanger's voice but Daphne appeared not to notice it.

"Well, are we going to discuss any more plans tonight?" she wanted to know. "Or shall we all go to bed? It's getting on toward an unholy hour and we none of us slept much last night."

"The only question is, shall I tell Inspector Fisk what Kent confided to me, or shall we make another attempt to reach the girl ourselves?" Before any of them could answer Faith again turned toward the open window. "There! I *did* hear something, it's Tibits!"

In fact the loud, distressed meowing of a cat came in from the terrace and Daphne, who happened to be nearest the window, leant out to call the animal's name.

"Listen, he's hurt or in trouble—why doesn't he come in?" As Faith started forward Sanger suddenly laid a detaining hand on her arm; there was something vaguely terrifying about the cat's continuous, high-pitched wailing. "Let me go, Murray, Tibits needs our help."

He released her arm as suddenly as he had grasped it, following her to the window where Daphne still leaned out, urgently calling. There was a scratching, scuffling sound on the gravel walk and in the instant that the great yellow cat leapt into the path of light streaming out from the window, Murray Sanger caught back the leaning girl, twitching her sharply aside so that it was Faith's arms and not Daphne's that received the squalling, terrified pet.

"Tibits, Tibits darling," she soothed, "oh, be careful!" For in the extremity of his fear the cat had sunk outspread claws into her shoulder, "What on earth can have happened to him? He was never like this before."

Under her caressing touch Tibits gradually quietened, still meowing piteously half under his breath.

"The brute's clawed you." Her brother pointed to several tiny blood stains that stood out against the pale chiffon covering her shoulders.

"Well, he didn't mean to, did you darling?" She carried her pet to a corner of the couch, crooning love-words as he snuggled closer into her sheltering arms. "But I do think you men ought to go out and try to find what frightened him so horribly."

Thus urged they turned on terrace and garden lights, exploring the nearby shrubbery and as much of the roof as they could see, but it was a slightly half-hearted proceeding in which neither man took any particular interest, and they had found nothing to account for the cat's terror when a cry from Daphne recalled them to the music room.

In the corner of the big couch Faith lay, queerly crumpled, her eyes glittering but utterly expressionless, a light foam on her lips.

"Faith!" With the single cry Sanger was across the room and kneeling to gather her into his arms. "She's fainted— do something—get some water, ammonia, anything!"

"It's more than a faint," Daphne's voice sounded crisp, unemotional, "look at her pupils, they're dilated twice their natural size. What we need is a doctor, is there one in the building, Myron?"

"Yes, two floors down."

"Get him—*quick!*"

The urgency of her tone sent him out of the room on a run. When he had gone she stood quite still for a second, then rang the service bell which Fargo answered so promptly that she realized he must have been waiting up for the family's return.

"Miss Stanwix is ill," she told him. "See that there's hot water, and ice, I don't know exactly what the doctor will need, but it's serious, you'd better rouse her father."

"Some bad liquor, I suppose, got in that infernal night club," Sanger groaned when Fargo, soft-footed as ever, had hurried away.

"No, I don't think it's that. We were all served from the same bottle and there's nothing wrong with the rest of us. I believe the cat's to blame."

"Tibits?" his voice held amazed incredulity. "Why he didn't bite her!"

"Stupid! His claws, not his teeth—" Daphne snapped at him. "I'm sure they were smeared with poison—the same hand that struck down the Cardigans, father and son, has struck again!"

"God!" He gathered Faith closer, as if to shield her from the invisible menace that struck and left no trace.

"Fargo told me—" Mark Stanwix hurried in clad in dressing gown and slippers, then stopped short at sight of the unconscious girl in Sanger's arms. "What's happened? Is she hurt?"

"Poisoned, I think." It was no time to mince words. "Myron's gone for a doctor; they're coming now."

A door slammed, the sound followed by a patter of running feet, and Myron dashed in closely followed by a half-dressed man carrying a physician's bag. Under his directions Faith was laid flat on the couch while he hastily examined glassy eyes and flickering pulse, then ordered her carried to her own room where she must be put to bed and proper treatment instantly begun.

"No." As Daphne offered her assistance. "I need a professional nurse, 'phone to the Flower Hospital for one—at once please. I can carry her alone if someone will kindly show me the way."

His glance flitted over them to settle on Mark Stanwix, who instantly led the way toward Faith's bedroom.

"He saw it was poison and—he doesn't trust us!" There was acute horror in Daphne's wide open yellow eyes. "That's why he wouldn't let me help! Well," She flashed round accusingly on Myron. "Why don't you go telephone the hospital? Why stand there wasting precious time?"

When he had rushed out again she turned blindly toward Murray Sanger.

"Oh, why did you pull me aside like that? Why didn't you let Tibits' claws poison *me* instead of Faith?"

"I don't know," he muttered sullenly. "There was a wild note in the cat's cry—and you were nearest—I caught you away on an impulse of fear."

"You're lying!" There was a strangled, sobbing laugh that rose in her throat and refused to be wholly stifled. "You did it because you love me—because if a danger threatened you thought of me first!"

"*No!*" he almost savagely denied.

"*Yes!* Why struggle, why pretend? You know it was destined—know we were mated the first time our eyes met."

"Treacherous!" he sneered at her.

"Am I? Or is it only for men that 'All's fair in love or war?'"

"Love? Much you known of love! You're gripped by pride of your beauty, by lust of conquest—you want to take me away from Faith, even now when she's close to Death's door!"

"You're wrong. It's the urge of terror that's ripped away pretense and lent me courage to speak the truth. If you weren't a coward you'd admit that our love is so big it's dwarfed everything else."

"A coward! I!" his harsh, rasping laugh held no trace of mirth. "You're the first who ever called me that!"

"Then prove your courage. Prove you're not afraid to face love, yours and mine! Take me now, when I'm frightened, into the safety of your arms."

"No," he refused. "You are only a fire in my blood, a delirium that will pass. I tell you it's Faith I love."

"Liar!"

With a movement so swift it permitted of no parrying she had covered the space between them, had wound her arms about him, hands locked behind his neck so that he could not free himself without actual roughness. Her whole supple body pressed close, while the velvet smoothness of her lips crushed themselves on his, then strayed caressingly up the lean line of his cheek until they were whispering softly, urgently, into his ear.

"No!" He appeared to cling frantically to that one denying monosyllable as to his only hope of safety. "No!"

"But yes! Yes!"

The fervid, heated whispering again murmured into his ear and quite suddenly the man's resistance snapped; she was crushed, blinded, almost stifled by the wild passion of his arms and lips. Yet even while she gave herself as prey to his devouring kisses Daphne's senses remained on guard, it was she who heard approaching voices, warning him in time so that they were decently apart when Faith's father and brother reentered the music room.

Myron had gone to his sister's door after calling the hospital, to report that a nurse would be sent immediately.

"The doctor had Fargo call one of the maids, she's helping him in the meantime; he wouldn't let me stay." The old gentleman sank wearily into a chair, leaning forward to clasp his head in both hands.

"But Faith—you haven't told us what the doctor says!" The breathless quality of Daphne's voice had the sound of keen anxiety; only Murray Sanger knew it was caused by something more than that.

"He's not saying much," Myron answered her question, "though he seems to think there's a faint hope Faith won't die. He says the claws passing through her dress is what may save her; the chiffon wiped off part of the poison before they entered her flesh."

"But why was it done? That's what I can't understand. Why should anyone want to kill little Faith?" The father lifted a haggard face to stare appealingly from one to the other.

"Perhaps it was meant to strike at you, through her," Sanger suggested.

"Even so, what have I done to incur such enmity? It's like some hideous nightmare. One death follows another with no reasonable motive, no one we can logically accuse!"

"Doesn't it all seem to center around whatever secret Peter Cardigan locked away in that safety deposit box?" Daphne went closer to the old man, her beautiful face showing a gentle sympathy, a desire to help, and not the faintest trace of eagerness.

"Yes, yes, I believe you're right." He was by now only too anxious to snatch at any hope of ending the strange reign of terror that enveloped his home, and the hurt to little Faith had struck so deep as to shake his normally arrogant self-confidence. "I had a certain reason which I prefer not to publish even now, for not wanting that box opened, but I admit I was wrong. I'll arrange to have Inspector Fisk meet me tomorrow, before the bank closes, and we'll open it together. Will you 'phone Whitney Page in the morning, Myron, and ask him to meet me at the bank at two o'clock? As the other executor of the Cardigan estate his presence will be necessary."

"But you'll be seeing him yourself before then, dad. Have you forgotten Peter Cardigan's funeral?"

"For the moment it had completely slipped my memory—I seem unable to think clearly about anything but Faith's danger." Then, with a sudden start, "What's become of the cat? We ought to make certain it doesn't scratch anyone else."

They had all of them forgotten Tibits and now that they tried to find him he appeared to have mysteriously vanished. It was Daphne who presently remembered the cat's fondness for sleeping on her bed.

He was there, but not asleep, for being a fastidious animal he had carefully cleaned his claws and the result was a stiff, furry corpse stretched on the silken counterpane.

15

FARGO DISAPPEARS

In the morning the doctor, who had remained all night with his patient, pronounced Faith out of danger.

"All she needs now is quiet and careful nursing," he told Mark Stanwix in answer to the latter's anxious inquiries. "The fact that her arms and shoulders were not quite bare is undoubtedly what saved her life; a portion of the poison adhered to the material and so failed to enter her blood."

"You are leaving the nurse in charge?"

"Yes, though I'll be back myself later in the day." He still lingered, evidently bitten by a curiosity which at length drove him into asking: "How did the cat manage to get this poison onto its claws? It was one of the aconitine alkaloids—used medicinally of course, though seldom in such strong potency; I find myself unable to understand how it came to be on the animal's claws."

"There I'm as much at sea as you are. I shall be glad to tell you the explanation if I ever learn it."

And with that the physician was obliged to rest content; since his patient's father firmly declined any further discussion of the subject.

When he had gone Mark Stanwix partook of a solitary breakfast, then telephoned police headquarters and rather to his surprise found Inspector Fisk already in his office.

He gave him a guarded version of what had happened, asking Fisk to come up for a conference at the penthouse as soon as possible.

"As you doubtless know, funeral services were held in the crematory chapel before Peter Cardigan's body was consigned to the flames, but today a few close friends intend seeing his ashes placed in the family vault. It's a kind of final tribute to a man we all loved and trusted, and one which I'm loath to forego paying; therefore if you find it convenient to come up here before we leave—there are several matters it might be well to discuss at this time."

The inspector promised to make it convenient, and, true to his word, arrived inside the stipulated hour, having collected Sydney Traherne on the way.

They were told in detail of the strange attack on Mr. Stanwix' daughter, made by means of her own pet cat.

"A devilish scheme, devilish!" Fisk was genuinely incensed. It was bad enough to kill men for no apparent reason, but to attempt murdering an innocent girl who could by no conceivable stretch of the imagination have injured anyone, seemed infinitely worse.

"Why so sure that the attack was actually meant for her?" Traherne inquired. "Mr. Stanwix tells us she wasn't alone."

"For whom else could it have been meant?" Their host eyed him with indignant scorn. "From what the young people tell me I judge whoever poisoned the cat's claws held him until his distressed cries drew Faith to the window, then released him knowing that badly frightened and probably hurt, he'd be bound to fly to her for protection and almost certainly sink his claws into her flesh in the frantic effort to cling tight to the person whom, to his feline mind, represented safety."

"Why wasn't the whole garden instantly searched?"

"Because at the time no one realized deliberate intention behind the cat's terror," Max Stanwix stiffly informed him. "It was only when the poison began to take effect that they realized the diabolical ingenuity which counted on a girl's love for her pet to destroy her. Though, as a matter of fact, I believe Murray Sanger and my son did try to discover what had frightened the cat before they suspected anything seriously wrong. Naturally once Faith's condition became apparent, they could think of nothing else."

"Very convenient for the would-be murderer, but in any case by that time he was probably well away."

"At least last night's affair proves what we've partially known all along," the inspector stated after a momentary pause. "Your enemy must possess free access to the roof."

"Granted. But why my enemy?" Mark Stanwix demanded. "What's the motive—how does the murderer benefit?"

"We may be able to answer that once we know the contents of Peter Cardigan's deposit box. Hasn't the attack on your daughter lessened your objection to opening it?"

"More than that, it's completely removed it, though the fact may be construed as a selfish weakness on my part; I am now as anxious as you are to have the box opened and at least part of this hideous mystery cleared away."

"Good. The sooner the better. Can it be done this morning?"

"Not this morning, I'm afraid. There won't be time before we leave for the Tarrytown cemetery. It will have to be early this afternoon, say two o'clock; if you'll arrange to be in my office in the bank at that time we can open it together."

"Very well. In the meantime I'll see about setting an efficient guard at all the entrances to the roof, and probably an officer had better be stationed in the penthouse itself."

"You can attend to all that by 'phone," Traherne unexpectedly cut in. "I think it might be a good idea for both of us to drive out to this ceremony in the Cardigan vault."

"Why? You're surely not anticipating trouble there?" Fisk eyed his friend with distinct surprise.

"Not trouble, perhaps, I shall simply feel safer if we keep Mr. Stanwix under our eyes as long as he carries that infernal key round in his own private pocket."

A discreet tap at the door prevented their pinning him down to a more definite statement. It was Fargo to say the building's superintendent was on the 'phone and anxious to speak with Mr. Stanwix. After only a short absence he returned, looking puzzled and a trifle annoyed.

"The superintendent reports that one of the office cleaning women is downstairs and insists on seeing me personally; she won't tell him her reason but hints she's discovered something about Peter Cardigan's murder."

"I hope you've had her sent up?"

"Yes. Though I doubt its more than a foolish suspicion the woman's somehow picked up."

It was the cleaning woman, Letty, whom they had questioned the day after the discovery of Peter Cardigan's body, but at that time she had professed complete ignorance of the tragedy while now she was swelled with a sense of the importance of her own news. She remembered both the inspector and Sydney Traherne; Mr. Stanwix she knew by sight though she had ever before spoken to him.

"You gentlemen put a lot of questions to me about last Saturday afternoon," she began, one scrubby red hand smoothing the skirt that was obviously her Sunday best. "There wasn't much I could tell you, seeing as Mr. Cardigan wanted me not to clean that day, account of him expecting a visitor—but last night a clew to who done the poor gentleman in fair fell in my hand, as you might say."

She stopped, savoring the full enjoyment of their rapt attention and loath to end it by imparting her news. Inspector

Fisk brought her back to earth by ostentatiously glancing at his watch, then remarking with official gruffness:

"Very interesting, my good woman, but we're in somewhat of a hurry. Better tell us your 'clew' without further wasting time."

"Ain't I telling it as fast as I can?"

"Well, out with it, what do you think you've discovered?"

"Maybe you'll remember me saying a man in a gray suit went into Mr. Cardigan's office and so far as I seen didn't come out of it, leastways not him before, but I'd a real good look at his face and knew if I was to see him again I'd surely know it. Well, last night showed I was right!"

"You've actually seen this visitor of Mr. Cardigan's again? You know who he is?" The inspector was conscious of a longing to shake the woman into more rapid speech.

"That I have, sir, and a terrible shock it was."

"Well, who is he?"

"If you'd let me tell how it come about, in my own way, sir." Letty evidently objected to being rushed and the fuming inspector realized that to give her free rein was the quickest way to learn what she knew; he lapsed into restive silence, allowing her to ramble happily on.

"There was a Chinee bowl as used to set on Mr. Cardigan's desk, and him putting flowers in it every now and then. It was an awful ugly thing, all over crawly snakes with legs to 'em but he set store by it and was cruel vexed when it kind of jumped out of me hands one night last week and got itself smashed."

Here the inspector cast a plaintive glance heavenward, as if imploring patience. What earthly connection had a Chinese bowl, broken while he was still alive, to do with Peter Cardigan's murder?

"Mr. Cardigan must have forgot to tell his sister about the bowl getting itself broke," Letty thus carefully disclaimed all blame in the matter, "because when I come on duty last night the superintendent tells me she was down to his office yesterday, a fussing on o'count of the bowl being broke. He didn't know nothing about it so she said I was to go up to her apartment so soon as I come to work last night and tell her what become of the bowl. Well, sir, I done that same, and after I'd seen Miss Cardigan and was waiting to be took down stairs again who should be getting out of the elevator but the man in the gray suit what I told you about. He didn't give me a look, just rung the Cardigans' bell and a maid let him in. I was that faint from seeing him again like that I couldn't hardly get in the elevator—but I come to and asked the man what runs it who he was."

"And he knew?" Poor Fisk could no longer curb his impatience.

"He did, sir; 'twas the gentleman what butlers for Mr. Stanwix!"

"Fargo! Is this true?" He swung to demand of Mark Stanwix. "Did Fargo go down to the Cardigan apartment last night?"

"Yes. I remember Faith sent some ice cream, a thing she often does."

"Ring for him!"

The suggestion was hardly needed, Stanwix' finger was already pressing the bell.

"You're certain it was the same man you saw entering Peter Cardigan's office last Saturday afternoon?" Fisk asked Letty while they waited for the bell to be answered.

"Certain sure, sir, no woman young or old could get mixed about a man with a face that beautiful, sir."

Which remark suggested that under certain circumstances masculine good looks may possess disadvantages.

"He's a thundering long time answering."

The inspector had started for the door when it opened to admit a slightly flustered maid.

"Where's Fargo?" he almost barked at her.

"I don't know, sir, that's why I answered the bell, hearing it ring so hard and not being able to find him."

"My God, the man's bolted!"

It was only too true, the handsome butler was missing. One elevator boy reported taking him down to the 19th floor, where he got off after asking if the boy knew whether Whitney Page was at home as Mr. Stanwix had sent him down with some papers which were to be given into the lawyer's own hands; in substantiation of which statement the boy said Fargo carried a small flat grip. After that no one remembered having seen him, though he had apparently left the penthouse hatless and wearing his butler's uniform.

Inspector Fisk set the official machinery to work broadcasting Fargo's description and the fact that he was badly wanted by the police, and, at Traherne's suggestion, a watch was set on the Panther's Den in case he went there, after which there seemed nothing more they could do.

Mr. Stanwix, his son, Murray Sanger and the detective gathered for a consultation in the library where they were presently joined by Whitney Page who declared Fargo had not been near his apartment.

"Does the man's flight mean a confession of guilt?" the dapper little lawyer wanted to know.

"I think so, but I'll admit uncertainty of precisely what kind of guilt, or what degree," Conway Fisk answered. "So far as we know he may be guilty of the first murder—he'd no particular alibi if you remember, simply claimed to have been on duty here in the penthouse. He may also have poisoned the cat's claws last night, and somebody told me he appeared, fully dressed, when the bell was rung—but as I see it he can't have killed Kent Cardigan."

"Why not?" Whitney Page was fidgeting about the room, his poise of bland benignity badly ruffled by Fargo's sudden flight and the conclusions to which it pointed. "Why not? If you remember he spoke over near the door which none of us heard open, while the room was still dark. Couldn't he have stolen in the very instant the lights went out, stabbed Kent, carried the knife out to some hiding place in the hall from which it could be removed at his leisure, and then returned with the lamp which he'd have prepared beforehand?"

"You're leaving out the cleaning of a knife in one of the flower beds, the dropped rope and the ladder."

"Not at all," Page flatly contradicted. "I think we've all along suspected there was more than one person concerned in these Cardigan murders. Besides, if Fargo's not guilty, why has he taken to his heels?"

"At present that's beyond me," the inspector admitted. "Also, I don't think I've said I believed the man innocent—in fact we, Traherne and I, have felt from the beginning there was something fishy about him and if I hadn't been so rushed I should certainly have had his record and references thoroughly looked into."

"You'll do that now, I suppose?"

"Of course, but it's a bit late in the day."

"It is, most decidedly." Whitney Page eyed him with a distinctly baleful glare, then lifted perfectly tailored shoulders in a contemptuous shrug. "Quite a striking example of the usual police method—always let your horse get stolen before you lock the stable door."

Ignoring the little man's rather spiteful criticism, the inspector quietly verified the two o'clock appointment at the Stanwix Bank, then he and Traherne left to attend some necessary business connected with the dragnet cast for the missing butler, before driving out to the Sleepy Hollow Cemetery in North Tarrytown.

16

THE PRIVATE ELEVATOR

The Cardigan family vault, stone faced and running deep into the grassy slope of a tree-embowered hill, was one of the oldest in the old Sleepy Hollow Cemetery. For generations the Cardigans had laid their coffined dead to rest in its dim silence, and they had been a prolific family, judging by the number of coffins that filled the original niches built into the masonry and those all tenanted, stood neatly aligned on the stone-paved floor itself.

Unlike many old families this one seemed not to have dwindled in size with the passing years, for since they had taken to cremation, either through lack of adequate space, or a desire to follow the newer fashion, there had apparently been many deaths; a long line of funeral urns designed to contain ashes, were ranged on a kind of shelf which had evidently been added to the tomb's original fittings.

The marble urn holding all that remained of Peter Cardigan was duly added to the somber row, and an old friend of his, a Minister of the Gospel, read the funeral service for the dead while the group of men, there were no women present, stood with doffed hats, gravely paying their last tribute to a man who had been universally respected.

No ghouls of the press attended the brief ceremony, indeed it was largely to avoid their attentions and consequent publicity that it had been arranged to take place at

such an early hour, and when it was over the little company filed out into the clear sunlight, soberly said good-bye,
and got into their several cars for the return drive to the
city.

Murray Sanger and Myron Stanwix were using the former's high-powered sports-model, a brilliantly colored
and metaled affair that looked oddly out of place in the
quiet, old-world cemetery, but Mark Stanwix had come
out in a dark blue limousine in which he suggested Fisk
and Traherne return with him, so that they could talk on
the way back to town.

"Sorry, sir, we have our own car," the inspector explained. "Also talking over the case won't do much good
until we know the secret of that safety deposit box. We'll
both be in your office at two sharp."

Once out on the Albany Post Road the various cars
separated, going their several ways at the speeds that best
suited their driver's tastes or abilities and by the time Traherne and the inspector had passed through Yonkers they
had lost sight of all the others.

Both men were rather silent, inclined to absorption in
their individual thoughts, and it was not until they had
swung west into the sweep of Riverside Drive that the
inspector remembered a bit of news which he had failed
to impart.

"By the bye, that operative I lent you last night is a
most conscientious soul; I found her waiting at headquarters when I turned up there at an unholy early hour this
morning."

"Was she able to trace the man I pointed out at the
Panther's Den?"

"Yes. Followed him home and late as it was found an
all-night Coffee Pot restaurant where they knew him and
weren't averse to passing the time with a bit of gossip.
The man's known as Andre Tretinto, supposed to be an

Italian, and owns a little antique shop dealing mostly in old metals, brasses, wrought irons, bronzes and the like—a good part of them cleverly forged by Andre's own hands, according to her Coffee Pot informant."

"So?" Traherne's tone expressed lively satisfaction but he offered no comment and the inspector presently asked if he wanted the metal-worker arrested.

"No, but I'd like one of your men to keep an eye on him; he's likely to prove a valuable witness."

There was another space of silence between them, broken by the inspector's aggrieved complaint:

"Sid, what's wrong with this case that you won't discuss it, or let me know your honest opinion? Why turn oyster over whatever suspicions you're nursing?"

"Because I've no evidence to back them up, and once our criminal scented danger God knows how many deaths might follow. If I told you what I know, and suspect, you couldn't resist taking instant action."

"How long am I to be kept in the dark?"

"Impossible to be sure—I'm hoping that I shall dare to speak frankly before today's over."

"At least tell me why, yesterday morning, you walked off with those potted tulips from the study."

"Sorry, it can't be done; they lie too close to the heart of our mystery." And not another word concerning the case would Traherne say.

They lunched, drove to headquarters to see if any news of the missing Fargo had come in during the inspector's absence, and learning that so far there was no trace of him, kept their two o'clock appointment at the Stanwix Bank.

Its president had earlier telephoned from the penthouse giving directions that, in case they arrived before he himself finished luncheon and came down, Inspector Fisk and whoever accompanied him were to be instantly admitted to his private office. Though it lacked only a minute or two of the appointed hour when a clerk showed them in to the president's office, its sole occupant was his secretary, a capable looking young woman who pulled forward a couple of chairs, explaining that Mr. Stanwix would immediately join them.

After that the second hand of the small brass desk clock raced off the seconds until they mounted into minutes, two o'clock, two-five, two-ten, and still nothing happened. Perhaps the inspector's nerves were not quite at their normal best, or his patience thinned by too much unproductive pondering over the case, at any rate he objected to being kept waiting and at ten after two announced the fact in no uncertain terms.

"We've something better to do than cool our heels while Mr. Stanwix dallies over his lunch. Kindly 'phone the penthouse, young woman, and ask how soon he intends coming down."

The secretary started to refuse, glanced at the inspector's heavily knitted brows and thought better of it; the penthouse call was made. In answer to the secretary's question a woman's voice stated that Mr. Stanwix had started down to the bank some little time before; which piece of information further upset the inspector's disposition when it was passed on to him.

"Here, let me do the talking." He relieved her of the telephone and spoke into it himself. "Inspector Fisk speaking. You say Mr. Stanwix's already started down here—I'm in his office at the bank—how long ago?"

"I'm not rightly sure, sir, I didn't see him go."

"Then what the devil did you mean by stating he was on the way down?"

"It's what he said, sir, going out of the dining room."

"You're one of the maids, aren't you?"

"Yes, sir."

"Well, go and look for Mr. Stanwix, he must be some-where up there—or if you can't find him send somebody to the 'phone who knows when he left and which way he came down."

"Yes, sir."

There was a little wait, then another voice, musically smooth, but faintly anxious, came over the wire.

"This is Daphne Fane. The maid tells me you are wait-ing in Mr. Stanwix' office and that he hasn't arrived there. I don't quite understand. He left here fully a quarter of an hour ago. Has she made some mistake?"

"He's not here. How did he come down?"

"I don't know. I suppose as always, by his private ele-vator."

"You didn't actually see him leave?"

"No. He and Whitney Page left the lunch table togeth-er, they were talking about their appointment with you."

"Please see if any of the maids know where he is, and ring back if they do.

Fisk replaced the instrument and turned, his blue eyes filled with an anxiety which the sight of Whitney Page just entering from the main portion of the bank did nothing to relieve.

"Where's Mark Stanwix?" he almost barked at the as-tounded little lawyer.

"Why—isn't he here?"

"No, and I'm told you and he left the penthouse to-gether."

"The dining room, not the penthouse," Page corrected. "As a matter of fact we parted company in the hall; I had to stop at my place for a necessary paper so couldn't come down with him, as his private elevator is a non-stop affair."

"Better open the private elevator at this end," Sydney Traherne's quiet voice cut across their somewhat heated tones. "Mr. Stanwix may have been taken ill on the way down."

There was an instant's ominous pause, as if all of them dreaded opening the polished mahogany door blankly facing them from a rear corner of the office. Then Traherne crossed to it and lifting the safety handle, slid the door wide open. Behind it was the plain little private elevator, its floor disfigured by the grotesquely sprawling body of a man who lay, face down, his head the center of a widening crimson pool.

"God! It's Stanwix!" With the cry Inspector Fisk, for once forgetful of a cardinal rule of his profession, turned the body completely over, revealing the set dead face of the man for whom they were waiting. "Suicide! He shot himself on the way down!"

There was no doubt as to the cause of death, a bullet had shattered his right temple, and another entered his breast just above the heart.

"Twice?" Traherne's cool voice inquired. "And if so, where's the gun?"

In fact the floor of the car was innocent of any weapon, while its scrolled metal sides were too narrowly patterned to permit of a revolver's falling outside the car. To make sure they lifted the dead bank president, carrying him to a long table in the office, and again examined the elevator floor; it was bare and shining except for the sinister pool of blood.

"Yet it can't be murder!" Fisk sounded a trifle dazed. "Once in that elevator he was shut off from the world, inside a solid cement shaft—how could anybody get at him."

"They couldn't, but they did," Traherne curtly retorted. "It's up to us to discover how it was managed." He turned to the white cheeked but still efficient secretary. "How long had you been here in the office before we came?"

"Since half past one."

"You heard no shot, no disturbance of any kind?"

"None."

"You know how to run this particular elevator?

"Certainly."

"Can it be started from the outside? I mean, could Mark Stanwix' dead body have been placed inside the car and someone else sent it down?"

"No," her negative was prompt and positive. "It's of the self-service kind that only starts when the person using it has gone inside and shut the door."

"Yet I had no trouble opening the door just now."

"Because of the car's being on this level. Had it been up at the penthouse the door would have remained locked until it came down."

"So." Traherne mentally balanced the utter impossibility of this new murder against the indisputable fact that it had nevertheless been somehow committed.

"And the murderer couldn't have started down with him and left the car after Stanwix was shot—there's no way for him to get out." The inspector was staring blankly into the elevator's empty, brightly lighted interior. He shook himself, the physical movement a half-conscious effort to shake off the bewildering fog blanketing his mind. "I suppose we daren't use it to run us up to the penthouse for fear of destroying fingerprints—though all things considered, I'm damned if I see how there can be any except Mark Stanwix' own. We'd better go through the hall elevator that runs to the apartment floors." Then to the secretary: "Are you afraid to carry on here alone? I'd like Mr. Page to wait in the outer office."

"No, I'm not afraid."

"Good girl! I'll 'phone headquarters to send a finger-print expert, photographer, and the coroner's physician. Don't let anyone else in before they get here."

Up in the Stanwix penthouse they found Daphne Fane alone, except for a group of rather frightened maidservants.

"I didn't call you back because none of them saw Mr. Stanwix enter the elevator, or can say where he went after leaving the dining room," she explained, then, realizing the set gravity of their faces, dismissed the maids and led the way to the library. "What's happened?"

"Another murder! Mark Stanwix was shot while on his way down to the bank."

"Oh!" The back of her hand was pressed, hard, against her eyes, then it dropped and she faced the two men with a certain chill rigidity.

"Then he didn't use the private elevator?"

"On the contrary—he was killed while inside it, alone."

"How is that possible?"

"It's not, but it happened," the inspector bitterly informed her. "You say none of the maids saw him part from Whitney Page, or enter the car?"

"No. The two simply left the dining room together, after that no one saw either of them."

"Where were you?"

"I went from the luncheon table directly to the music room."

"Alone?"

"Yes."

"Where's Myron Stanwix?"

"I don't know, at least not definitely. He 'phoned in from somewhere in the Bronx to say he and Murray Sanger had caught a glimpse of a man they thought was Fargo going into some store out there—they'd parked the car and were cruising round on foot trying to find the man and make sure."

"How long ago was this?"

"Why—about half an hour, I think. We were at the luncheon table. Perhaps Ellen, the maid who answered, and called Mr. Stanwix to the 'phone, can remember more definitely."

When sent for Ellen was able to tell them that Myron Stanwix had telephoned at 1:35—she had noticed the time while passing through the hall on her way to the dining room.

"Why didn't the young folks call headquarters if they thought they'd seen Fargo?" the inspector fumed when the girl had gone out again.

"I don't know. Mr. Stanwix came back to the table and told us what Myron had just said, that's all I can tell you."

"'Us' being Whitney Page and yourself?"

"Of course. Faith is still in bed. Oh dear! I shan't dare tell her about her father, the shock might do serious harm, though the doctor feels sure she's quite out of danger."

"Better not tell her yet," Fisk advised. "We're going back to the bank now, if Myron comes home send him down at once."

"Before we go—I'd like asking Miss Fane a question," Traherne said slowly. "Can you tell me who the pot of yellow tulips in the study belonged to?"

"Why yes," she eyed him with narrow-lidded surprise, "they were mine."

"A gift?"

"No, I bought them myself."

"When?"

"On Monday."

"And they were in the study from then, until Kent Cardigan died there?"

"Why—yes."

"Thanks. That's all I wanted to know."

17

ON THE TWENTIETH

"Now, putting official red tape and estate executor's scruples aside, it's time we opened that safety deposit box." Inspector Fisk straightened from a brief search through the dead man's pockets. "Here's the key."

The bank manager, who had been called in and told of the new tragedy directly they returned from the penthouse, offered no objection; in fact he suggested going with them to smooth any difficulties over the breaking of rules and regulations. As a discreet after-thought Whitney Page in his capacity of the sole surviving executor of Peter Cardigan's will, was added to the little party bent on at last opening the mysterious deposit box that apparently formed the storm center round which raged so much ruthless passion of greed, hate, or fear; none of them knew quite which.

It was with a slightly unsteady hand that Inspector Fisk—all necessary formalities duly complied with—at length fitted the key into its individual lock. Another second and they would know what the box contained. Then the small heavy door swung wide and a gasp of mingled rage and astonishment escaped his tight-set teeth—the box was empty except for an impudent, cleverly drawn sketch of a sleek black panther squatting on a tombstone, its sharp-fanged mouth stretched in a leering, self-satisfied grin.

"The Devil! He's beaten us to it!" Fisk cursed softly but whole-heartedly under his breath.

"But the key! How'd he get the key?" Whitney Page squeaked, impotently dancing about on the tips of his small dapper toes.

"I don't know. Unless it was taken from the office, and used, while we were upstairs."

"It wasn't! No one went in or out of the office while you were gone! I was sitting just outside and never once took my eyes off the closed door."

"Then he's somehow obtained a duplicate." Fisk swung to the shock-numbed manager. "You're in authority here and know the ropes—find out what's happened."

It had been the inspector's intention to keep the news of its president's murder a secret until after the bank's usual closing time—now only a matter of minutes away— but under stress of a rifled safety deposit box on top of an unexplainable murder the manager lost his head and began questioning all and sundry, so that news of Mark Stanwix' violent death spread through the bank, causing something in the nature of a panic.

No one was able to throw the slightest light on how unauthorized access to Peter Cardigan's deposit box had been obtained, both the bank employees on guard at the vault's entrance insisted that no one had passed them without first presenting proper credentials, and neither could remember the entrance of any strangers.

"Of course, a good many people pass us going in and out," the elder of the two, a grizzled, heavy-jowled man of fifty explained to Inspector Fisk. "But the bank's checking system is very strict—anybody entering the vaults has to present one of our slips to prove they've a box belonging to them, or if they're sent by someone else they have to show the box owner's written authority. In that way, see-ing their names every time they come, we get to know most of the people using our vaults by sight. I believe I should remember if any stranger had come in today, and I can't recall seeing anybody I don't know."

Here Traherne drew the inspector aside for a low-voiced comment. "Aren't we wasting time with these men? After all we can't be certain how long the murderer's owned his duplicate key, or precisely when he used it."

"You're right, of course, though I'm so infernally mixed that the point hadn't occurred to me." He considered the new angle, adding: "Likely as not Peter Cardigan had a second key to the box on him when he was killed—and if so, the murderer had all this week in which to use it. Perhaps it was to delay discovery of the robbery that Kent Cardigan was stabbed."

They went back to the private office leaving the bank manager to pursue his inquiries alone. It was three o'clock by then, and the men from headquarters had been busy in the office for some little time. True to Fisk's prediction, the fingerprint expert reported no prints in the elevator interior other than Mark Stanwix' own. The medical examiner had just given permission for the body's removal when the door burst open and Myron Stanwix dashed in, closely followed by Murray Sanger.

"Is it true? Has dad been shot?" he demanded through shaking lips.

There was no need to answer, Myron had seen his father's body stretched on the table and with a strangled cry, flung himself down beside it, gripping the senseless arm in frantically clutching fingers.

"Dad! Dad! Can you ever forgive me? I've been blind, mad, a fool!"

"Steady, lad." The inspector laid a firm but kindly hand on his heaving shoulder. "Don't lose your grip. You've your sister to think of now. Snap out of it."

"Oh, my God! You don't understand!" Myron shook off the encouraging hand and desperately clung to his father's body, his own racked by wild sobs. "I thought he was guilty! All these days I thought he'd killed Peter Cardigan and afterward Kent!"

"What!" They could none of them quite believe their own ears. "You honestly believed your father the murderer we were searching for?"

"Yes, and you'd have believed it too, if you'd heard the quarrel between them that I did." Myron was suddenly on his feet, defiantly facing them. "Dad had learned something about his old friend that he called illicit, disgraceful—if it wasn't stopped dad meant putting an end to it himself, so I heard him say. They stormed and raged at each other, I'd never heard either of them swear before and I think that's partly why I listened—too confused to realize what I was doing until I'd heard dad threatening Peter Cardigan in a way that, later on, when Uncle Peter was found dead, I couldn't forget. I watched him, I couldn't help it, and dad wasn't himself; he was hiding something. I was horribly afraid I knew what it was. Do you wonder that now, when whoever killed Uncle Peter has killed dad as well, I can't forgive myself that disloyalty?"

"You should have told the police about this quarrel," Fisk gravely reproached him.

"Yes, but I didn't dare," Myron confessed, "for fear of involving dad in case he was guilty."

"You'd best make amends by telling as much as possible about the quarrel now."

"Sorry—there isn't any more. I only gathered what I've already told you, that dad had learned some disgraceful fact about Uncle Peter and was threatening him with dire consequences if he didn't do as dad wished."

"You must have got some notion what your father had discovered."

"I didn't, not a glimmer," Myron earnestly denied.

The inspector could get nothing more out of him, and when he realized that fact, took up another angle.

"Well, suppose you two give an account of yourselves. Where have you been all this time?"

"Chasing phantoms," it was Sanger who answered, Myron having suddenly cast himself into a chair and buried his face in both hands to avoid seeing his father's body carried away.

"What type phantom?"

"Fargo. Coming back from the cemetery we swung across, heading for the east side of town, and suddenly thought we saw him dodging into a department store. Couldn't very well drive in after him so we parked the car and chased him on foot."

"No success, of course?"

"No need of rubbing it in," Sanger retorted, with a shadow of his engaging grin. "We're not fancying ourselves as sleuths—probably it takes special training."

"At what time did you see this man you thought was the missing butler?"

"Somewhere around one—shouldn't you say, Myron?"

Thus appealed to Myron looked up and cast a relieved glance at the now empty table.

"A bit after one, say ten minutes after. I know I'd seen a clock a little while before and noticed the time because I was getting hungry."

"Yes. Well, it's now after three—did you hang around a department store for nearly two hours?"

"It took a good half hour to drive down here," Myron aggrievedly reminded him. "And besides we weren't in the store all that time. A fat woman with about fifteen children and some pet dogs got in between us so we had to hunt each other as well as Fargo. I don't quite know what happened to Murray, but I got stifled and left the store,

saw a 'phone booth sign and rang up the house to say I'd
be late for lunch, then went back to Murray's car thinking
he'd make for that when he couldn't find me inside the
store. I'd forgotten just where it was parked so hunted
around a while, was overtaken by such violent pangs of
hunger that I ducked in a drug store for a malted milk—
we afterwards found that while I was drinking it Murray
had been back to the car and gone away again looking for
me—I was there the next time he had a look, and after that
we drove straight here, remembering that Uncle Peter's
deposit box was to be opened at two o'clock and it was
already nearly three."

"Very muddling proceeding from beginning to end,"
was Fisk's unflattering comment. "You should have called
a police officer the instant you thought you saw Fargo."

"Rot! Whoever saw a policeman when they wanted one?
If we'd caught Fargo you'd be singing quite a different
tune." Which was true enough to temporarily silence the
inspector's criticism.

A little later Traherne again drew his friend aside; this
time to say he wanted the private office cleared and the
death-car taken up to the penthouse and kept there, so
that he could get at the bottom of the elevator shaft which
its present position blocked.

The shaft bottom had been left in the cluttered, roughly
finished condition common to such portions of a big
office building as are expected to be seen only by the eyes
of working men. Traherne climbed down to it through the
forcibly propped open elevator door in the office, and was
gone so long that Fisk presently called down to know if
there was anything wrong.

"Depends on the point of view," his friend called back.
"I'll be through in a couple of minutes now."

It was longer than that, but he did presently climb out
of the shaft carrying something wrapped in a decidedly
soiled handkerchief.

"Ingenious devil, this murderer of ours," he muttered, carefully placing the bulging handkerchief on a nearby desk. "I still don't quite see how he managed it, but I intended finding out."

Fisk eyed the small untidy bundle with fervent interest. "What's inside?"

"Take a look."

He did so—his first comment a long, surprised whistle. "Two badly flattened bullets and some fresh-looking bits of plaster. What's the answer, Sid?"

"Somebody shot at Mark Stanwix from outside the car and those two bullets hit the metal scrollwork of which it's made instead of passing through an opening in the pattern and striking the man inside."

"But man, it couldn't be done!" Fisk expostulated. "The shaft runs solid from top to bottom of the building and the elevator doors, both here and at the penthouse, are of solid wood."

"Quite. But you haven't considered the plaster."

"I'm past considering anything!" the inspector feelingly complained. "I've never put in such a week in all my years on the force! And primarily it's all your fault. If you hadn't dragged me to that picture show and insisted on noticing what went on at an upper window instead of watching a patriotic parade, some other inspector might have been assigned to the case."

"Don't grouse. You know it would break your heart to have anyone else handling a case with as many impossible quirks as this one. And getting back to that plaster—I want a long rope, a short board, and a couple of husky men; might be as well to add some kind of pulley to the list."

"What the deuce for?"

"The rope to lower me down the shaft, board to sit on during the descent, men and pulley to do the real work. And," as an afterthought, "also a folding footrule."

The inspector's men had paid out only a comparatively short length of the rope when Traherne called up to hold it there. One of then, peering down into the shaft, could see his flashlight playing over one of the side walls, then a moment later they were told to pull him up—very slowly.

Back at the penthouse level he studied the footrule, making some sort of mental calculation, then asked Inspector Fisk to accompany him down the stairway leading to the apartment floors.

On the twentieth he turned from the stairway itself, walking slowly around an angle and along a short hall. When it turned he stopped to study a closed door, shook his head, then suddenly darted to one a little further along and tried it to see if it was locked; it was.

"Sorry to 'burgle' under your official eyes, old dear, but it has to be done."

He shamelessly produced that forbidden article, a skeleton-key, and fitting it into the lock swung the door wide. Inside was a crowded, rather disorderly storage room filled with trunks, cases, old lamps, all sorts of odds and ends belonging to various tenants. Pausing an instant to get his bearings Traherne pushed a way through the heterogeneous mixture to a breast-high opening in the wall where plaster and cement had been cut away, leaving a fair-sized hole that showed black as they looked at it from the lighted store room.

"That opens into the shaft of Mark Stanwix' private elevator," Traherne very gravely explained. "Of course the flattened bullets and fresh plaster at the shaft foot led me to expect something of the kind. When your men lowered me I found it easily enough and while they pulled me up, measured the distance and calculated it must be on this floor. Look."

He pointed to where a bucket of fresh plaster and a pot of paint of the same shade as the storage room's walls, sat, partly hidden behind a pulled-out trunk. "If we'd given the Panther a little more time he'd have patched up the hole so no one would ever be likely to find it. He probably reasoned it was wisest not to risk closing it up today—too many curious people all over the building—and he hardly expected us to figure out how Mark Stanwix was killed quite so soon."

"You called the Panther an ingenious devil—my God! He's a fiend! How did he ever think out such a way of shooting at a man I'd have sworn was temporarily safe from the most determined killer?"

"Clever, you know, at that. Notice how carefully he chose a spot which the elevator would pass slowly enough to give a chance for aiming? Lower down it would have been going too fast, here it hadn't gained its full momentum. Though even at that the Panther must be a decidedly skilled marksman."

"And to think that after three dastardly murders we've got no real clue to his identity, and damned little hope of catching him!"

"Oh, it's not quite *that* bad. Like most other criminals he's been guilty of one or two errors of judgment—I fancy they're nearly due to trip him up."

18

The Funeral Urns

Daphne Fane stood before the long mirror in her bed-room, wide opened golden eyes staring into its depths, but it was not the image of her own reflected loveliness that held her fascinated gaze—the mirror showed a man's hand grasping the curtain of a window behind her, and a little to one side.

Very slowly she turned, taking an uncertain step toward the window, beautiful strained eyes in which lurked a dawning terror fixed now on the hand itself instead of its mirrored reflection. Another wavering step and a man's muted voice spoke softly—the fear died from her eyes and with a soft little rush she was close against the curtain.

"You! What's happened? Why are you here?"

The man's voice spoke rapidly, urgently, still in that muted undertone and Daphne silently listened, her flame-crowned head now and then nodding a quick understanding and compliance. Then the murmuring whisper ceased and the hand was gone.

Daphne remained for a little space without moving, perhaps listening for any sound outside, perhaps thinking over the just received instructions. A gong sounded somewhere in the depths of the house, and with an impatient little shake Daphne cast off the spell of inaction that held her. One hurried glance at the glass to be sure her dress and hair were in perfect order, then she switched off the light and obeyed the gong's call to dinner.

Later in the evening, a good deal later, Inspector Fisk sat forlornly at the desk in his office at police headquarters. Three murders—not even counting that of the insignificant bondsalesman, Roberts, which after all might, just conceivably, have been an accident—and no tangible clew to the clever devil, male or female, who had planned and executed them.

Could Fargo be guilty? Some evidence went to confirm, some to refute the possibility and his flight, if cast in with the former, heavily weighed the balance against his innocence. Yet could he, a hunted fugitive, his description broadcast far and wide as that of a man wanted by the police, have dared to enter the Stanwix building, cut through into the elevator shaft, and deliberately shot Mark Stanwix at the very moment when the police themselves were waiting for his coming? It was hardly conceivable, and yet, was it?

No one remembered seeing Fargo again after the elevator boy let him off at the 19th floor. Might he not have gone to earth in some secret, already prepared hiding place in the great building and never left it at all?

Of course Myron and Murray Sanger believed they had seen Fargo in the Bronx, but they might easily be mistaken, and as there had not been sufficient time to thoroughly canvass all the Stanwix building's tenants an unidentified friend and accomplice of the vanished butler might lurk somewhere among them.

He was beginning to feel slightly cheered by thought of the new angle of inquiry thus suggested when the telephone on his desk shrilled so violently that he jumped.

"Yes. Inspector Fisk speaking."

Sydney Traherne's voice answered him. "I've been a blithering idiot, Fisk! Hop a taxi and come to my place as quick as you can make it. Hurry, we may still be in time!"

He found Traherne already seated in his car outside the apartment building where he lived, and its engine started almost before Fisk was safely inside. They shot away, headed uptown, at a pace that showed Traherne's abiding faith in a kindly Providence, or in the presence of a police official beside him.

"What's up?" Fisk demanded as they slid through a narrow opening in the traffic with not an inch to spare and brazenly stole a block after the lights had changed. "What's suddenly bitten you, and where are we going?"

"To the Sleepy Hollow Cemetery."

"Ye gods and little fishes—why?"

"Use your head, man, show you're not the blind bat I've been up to twenty minutes ago."

"Mind illustrating? The Sleepy Hollow Cemetery suggests nothing but well-regulated funerals to my befuddled brain."

"Remember that sketch of a grinning panther sitting on a tombstone left in the safety deposit box, and those lines of Cs scratched on Peter Cardigan's blotter—then, if you don't get any connection think about it, and don't talk—I need all my wits for driving."

They were twice stopped by irate police officers before the car fled along the comparatively deserted road beyond Tarrytown. Each time Fisk was able to convince the officers that they were travelling on police business too important for respect of speed regulations.

Opposite the high iron gates of the cemetery Traherne slowed to a crawl, nosing along until he found a lane on the west side of the post road. He swung into it, shut off the engine and lights, then descended and with a whispered, "Come on—quietly," led the way to a spot conveniently shadowed by overhanging trees.

There they shamelessly climbed the stone wall separating the Albany Post Road from the sleeping city of the dead. It was a moonless night, further darkened by banks of scurrying clouds that shut off the stars, and as Fisk stumbled along, barking his shins against unseen tombstones or ornamental urns he wondered how on earth Traherne knew the way—he was certainly following no prescribed path.

Far back in the depths of the quiet graveyard they paused, Traherne's detaining hand on the inspector's arm. They stole forward with redoubled caution across well-kept sward that felt soft and smooth to the feet. Not until heavy bronze doors loomed directly ahead did Fisk recognize the family vault of the Cardigans.

Instead of venturing a light Traherne's sensitive fingers felt along the bronze leaves, then he swore softly under the edge of his breath; the doors were ajar.

"Thanks to my stupidity we're too late," his tone held bitter self-disgust. "Too bad Whitney Page isn't here. He'd take joy in marking that it's not only the police who lock a stable after the horse's exit. Come on inside."

He deliberately pulled the door wide open and when they had slipped inside swung the heavy bronze leaf back into place, then switched on his powerful electric torch. The vault interior was as they had seen it that morning— with one glaring exception. Of the long row of urns that had stood on a shelf against the wall only Peter Cardigan's and one other remained intact; all the rest lay smashed to fragments on the stone paving. Inspector Fisk was too dazed for any comment, he simply stared at Traherne, dumbly demanding the reason.

"The Panther's evidently gifted with a sardonic sense of humor, he left that sketch as a clue to what he intended doing next, banking on our not connecting the tombstone it showed with the secret the deposit box revealed to him; of course he didn't know we'd a second clue in the shape of those curly-cues on the blotter."

"May be a clue to you, it says nothing at all to me."

"That's because you haven't given enough attention to Peter Cardigan's business—" Traherne was beginning when a sudden sound outside the vault made him shut off his light and stand listening, Fisk within touching distance of his arm.

Very slowly the vault doors swung open, framing two dimly seen shapes that stole in, half crouching. Another second and Fisk would have hurled himself at the invaders but just in time to prevent, one of them flashed on a torch and by its light they found themselves looking into the muzzles of two steadily held automatics backed by a voice that sharply ordered:

"Hands up!"

Fisk could feel Traherne's fingers close on his arm, but remained uncertain if they signaled obedience or attack— while he hesitated there was a scurrying, scuffling noise in the vault corner to the left of the door and slightly behind the newcomers—the light of the torch swung to cover the unexpected sound, showing a man's figure as it leaped erect and shot through the open door into outer darkness.

"Fargo!"

The amazed cry was wrung from the inspector's lips, to be answered by an oddly familiar laugh.

"Ye gods! Was it you I was ordering to 'up hands', inspector?" questioned an unmistakable voice. "Of course it was Fargo we were after."

"Murray Sanger!"

"The same, also Myron Stanwix. As you see we've been privately sleuthing again. Picked up Fargo's trail and followed him out here, but lost time parking the car so didn't arrive until you'd followed him in—or were you here first?"

"No, he was first on the scene. He must have heard us coming and dropped flat behind that coffin before we showed a light; there was no one visible then."

"Sorry if our turning up cramped your style," Sanger apologized. "I suppose there's no use hunting the cemetery for him now?"

"Not a particle, we might as well all drive home and go to bed. And see here, you two—" his voice was suddenly stern, "the next time you plan a private chase kindly let me know. It looks as if you'd let Fargo slip through your fingers twice today."

"Sorry," Sanger again repeated, but without much real contrition. "Our picking him up tonight was pure chance—we'd no time to get in touch with you."

"Anything more you want here?" the inspector asked Traherne and was told that he would like all three of them to go outside for ten minutes; at the end of which time he promised to join them.

Alone in the vault he turned on his light and kneeling, commenced searching amid the scattered fragments of the broken urns. It was some few minutes before he found what he was looking for; a torn scrap of paper to which some flakey white crystals still adhered. With the utmost care it was wrapped in a twist of tissue paper and stowed in the depths of his wallet. After a little more, this time unrewarded, crawling over the stone pavement, Traherne rose, dusted the knees of his trousers, and with a last glance around the vault went outside.

Inspector Fisk, who was waiting alone, explained that the others had grown impatient and gone off to Sanger's car.

"Just as well, we'll drive more slowly on the way back—there are one or two things that need talking over."

"Before you trot out any new theories, or clues that need discussing, I'd like being told what's behind tonight's expedition and what that Panther sketch and the curly-cues on Peter Cardigan's blotter had to do with it," Fisk remarked when the car had left North Tarrytown behind and was fairly headed for New York.

"Don't think I've intentionally kept you in the dark for sake of playing a lone hand," Traherne's pleasant voice held the note of half shy affection sometimes heard between two close, but undemonstrative friends. "As a matter of fact I've been groping in a good bit of darkness myself, with no more than one or two threads that I dared trust not to lead me into a still deeper maze. If you've sufficient patience I'd like going back to last Sunday when, thanks to the news reel camera, we found Peter Cardigan lying dead in his office.

"Even that early in the case I caught a peculiarity of the office that troubled me enough to persistently stick in my thoughts; there weren't as many books or letter files as there should be in a business office of that nature and the safe itself contained almost no stocks or bonds—though of course the latter might easily enough have been stolen by the murderer.

"That same day the Cardigan maidservant told us about numerous visitors, both men and women, who came to the apartment at night, very quietly. They were supposed to call on business but if so, why the apartment? why not the office during normal business hours? Right there one caught a hint of something underhand about Peter Cardigan's activities and nothing that afterwards occurred cleared away that impression.

"His stenographer declared a large sum of money was missing from the safe but said nothing at all, even when questioned, about missing securities of any sort. Next, one of the firm's outside bond salesmen fell victim to unexplained panic and took to his heels, presumably after reading the newspaper accounts of his employer's death. Why? He must have been personally guiltless, otherwise news of the old gentleman's murder wouldn't have come as a shock; then why such precipitous flight?

"He didn't even wait to collect the bag left at the hotel but vanished carrying only a briefcase under his arm—a case which failed to materialize when Roberts' body was afterwards found. What became of it—and would its contents, if found, have explained both Roberts' flight and the mysterious visitors who called at Peter Cardigan's apartment instead of his office? I trust you're beginning to see daylight along that particular line, old dear?"

"Devil a ray," Fisk retorted, sotto voce. "But go on, for the present I'm no more than a pair of attentive ears."

Before complying Traherne slowed up to offer his cigarette case, and light one himself.

"Next we hear of a quarrel serious enough to keep her brother awake—Myron tells us, now, that it was with his father and concerned a shameful fact he'd learned about his old friend. Items starting to click?"

"There's the beginning of a whir," Fisk acknowledged. "Go on, tell it your way."

"Taken together our facts strongly suggest that Cardigan's stock and bond firm was no more than a cloak covering some less respectable business, and in America today, we've only two man-sized rackets to choose from—bootlegging and drugs. There seemed nothing to indicate the former, no out-of-town house or factory where liquor could be conveniently stored, no delivery trucks, and no hint of a connection with Canada. On the other hand the books showed a startling number of entries for customs charges and the stenographer's explanation that they were for imported curios failed to carry conviction. Most antiquities are over a hundred years old and once they've reached that age come in free of duty.

"One could hardly avoid suspecting that the charges covered consignments of drugs that had been cleverly slipped through the customs concealed in some innocent article of trade. Then, supposing Peter Cardigan to be a

wholesale drug importer and distributer, his string of unobtrusive evening visitors was readily explained by the
supposition that they were the means by which the illicit
stuff was distributed among retail customers."

"That despatch case carried by Roberts, then, also
ceased to be a puzzle—drugs don't take up a great deal
of space. He was doubtless carrying enough to be worth a
small fortune and when news of Cardigan's murder reached
him before he'd had time to leave it with the various retail
dealers for whom it was meant, he would naturally get rid
of it as quickly as possible, fearing the illicit nature of
their business would come to light once matters were in
the hands of the police. Think I'm right so far?"

"Very likely, but it gets us no nearer finding out who
killed the old gentleman—and the others."

"For that I think it'll be necessary to try and reconstruct
the last day of Peter Cardigan's life. How long he'd been
dealing in drugs we've no means of guessing, but evidently
his old friend Stanwix only recently found out what was
going on. We've Miss Camellia's and Myron Stanwix' word
that there was a quarrel—and from the latter's story we
can feel fairly sure that Stanwix threatened him with expo-
sure unless the disgraceful business was given up. Which
also explains Stanwix' reluctance to having the deposit box
opened; he feared his dead friend's good name would suffer.

"Thus, last Saturday morning, we have Peter Cardigan
more or less upset by the quarrel and the threat, even
before he received at luncheon time the letter, or rather
drawing, which his sister tells us thoroughly terrified him.

"Considering the sketch of a panther used by way of a
signature in the note directing Kent Cardigan to surrender
the key to his father's deposit box without using it, and
the similar sketch later found in the box itself, I think
we're justified in concluding that the drawing received by
Peter Cardigan came from the same person.

"Miss Camellia insists there was nothing written, but there may have been a line or two which escaped her hurried glance, or the black border on paper and envelope may have carried their own message to the recipient. At least we're certain that it further upset him and that he repeatedly tried to reach Kent by 'phone.

"Failing, he apparently wrote to his son, perhaps a confession, perhaps a plea for help in a sudden emergency, we'll probably never know which as the murderer found and destroyed the letter before our arrival on the scene. But whatever else it contained, the letter didn't reveal what was in the safety deposit box. That is pretty well proved by the fact that the murderer, after thoroughly going through the office including the safe, risked capture by continuing the search in Peter Cardigan's study and later in his car."

"You haven't condescended to mention what he was looking for."

"A clew to the whereabouts of a large secret store of cocaine or other drug—a clue which he gained today when he succeeded in robbing Peter Cardigan's deposit box and by way of a jeer at our incompetence, left that insolent sketch of the grinning panther. Of course he would never have done that little thing had he known that on Saturday afternoon Cardigan—the secret of his hidden drugs heavy on his mind—absent-mindedly scratched a portion of the urns in his family vault on the desk blotter.

"It was the memory of those little curly-cues resembling a series of Cs, taken with the sketched panther sitting on a tombstone, that finally told me they actually represented the handles on the funeral urns—the large number of which had puzzled me during this morning's ceremony in the vault. Unfortunately I didn't wake up soon enough to prevent their being smashed and their contents falling into the Panther's hands. Among the fragments I found a few cocaine crystals sticking to a scrap of paper that had been dropped and overlooked."

"Great Horn Spoons! There must have been twenty of those urns!" the inspector wailed. "If they were even reasonably filled, or a decent quantity in each, they'd hold a tremendous fortune."

"Exactly. A fortune well worth committing murder for."

"But the Panther himself? Was he Cardigan's partner, do you think, or his enemy?"

"It's not possible to say with absolute certainty, though that vanity-case found in Cardigan's room points to a friendly connection. It was new, bought for some woman, and unsuitable as a gift for any of the three we find in his life—Miss Camellia would never use such a thing, it was too garish for Faith and too costly for his stenographer. Therefore, remembering the Panther Cub's liking for black and white we're fairly safe in supposing it was intended for her, in which case Cardigan and the Panther must have been friends or at least associates."

"Then why the murders, if the two were working together?"

"Lord, man, I've no key to what went on inside the mysterious Panther's head!" Traherne remonstrated. "I'm not even certain that I've correctly guessed his identity and if I have, there's no evidence to back the guess. The reason I wanted to go this far into the case with you, now, is because I intend going to the Panther's Den tonight and—well, if I have the bad luck to be caught I doubt having another chance to enlighten you."

"Sid, you can't do it! The risk's too great. At least let me go along."

"No," Traherne refused. "Last night Mitza half promised to talk more freely if I went back there tonight. If you were with me she'd shut up like a clam. Besides the

Panther himself never openly visits the place, so there's next to no danger of my running into him if I discreetly stick to the supper room and don't go poking about in the club's inner regions."

"I don't like it," the inspector fumed. "I don't like it at all. And what's more I won't let you risk your life—that's what it amounts to—without taking some precautions. If you won't let me go with you I'll take a squad of picked men and watch outside."

"Right. So long as you don't spoil my chances of getting Mitza to talk by rousing her suspicions."

"There's plenty of cover in that neighborhood and it's a dark night anyhow—don't worry about their seeing us."

19

"Daphne's Missing!"

It was already late when Sydney Traherne, in his guise of the slightly inebriated patron hopelessly enamored of the Panther's Cub, took his place at a table not too far from the main entrance.

The black and white specialty was already in progress but, unlike the other times when he had watched it, Mitza had only one dancing partner instead of two. The place of the tall, fantastically costumed negroes being taken by a slender man in black satin that fitted, glove like, covering hands, feet, even his neck, while his face itself was hidden behind a black-fringed mask.

The effect, under the single white ray which, as always, alternately dimmed and glared in rhythmic time with the jungle dance, was oddly unreal, oddly beautiful, but it was not the artistry of the two slim shapes, one black, one white, that caught at the breath in Traherne's throat—it was the crowning touch of the man's strange costume; the fanged, snarling head of an animal mounted capwise above his own. It was the Panther himself who danced!

As realization came to Traherne it brought with it a sickening discouragement; the club owner's presence there tonight seemed to disprove all his carefully built-up theories, for were the Panther the person whom he suspected, that shadowy incarnate mystery haunting the background

of the case should now be elsewhere—and very differently
occupied.

Dumbly watching, Traherne suddenly became aware of
an uneven quality in the throbbing beat of the light; the
intervals of darkness had lengthened as the dance neared
its climax. He wondered if it was the result of intention
or of something gone wrong with the lamp's mechanism.

The interpretation of female flight and male pursuit,
culminating in delayed capture, was differently rendered
tonight than when the negroes danced with the Panther's
Cub. With them one was slain, the other bore the jungle
girl away on stiffly extended arms but there was no em-
brace; the capture was symbolized rather than enacted.

Tonight the ending was different. The superbly graceful black dancer caught her elusive white slenderness in
strongly possessive arms, holding her as the two seemed
to blend in a moving ecstasy of love set to music. Traherne saw his lips fasten, through the hanging fringe of his
mask, on her throat and cling there while the dance flowed
smoothly on. Then slowly, very slowly, as if reluctant to
relinquish the slender woman-shape, he lowered her still
in time to the music, until she lay stretched, the black
dancer kneeling above her. A second the pose was held,
then the Panther gained his feet with one lithe bound and
danced triumphantly away leaving the girl stretched motionless just as he had laid her down.

It was an effective finish and in the shifting, uncertain
light even those nearest failed to notice a certain unnatu-
ral stillness about the prone white shape until a crimson
stain spreading down over the silk-clad shoulder drew a
horrified cry from some woman sitting close to the dance-
floor edge. "Look! It's blood!"

Next instant a dozen people were crowding round the
Panther's Cub, waiters, patrons, chattering voluble comments and advice. Traherne, throwing aside all pretense of

drunkenness, pushed a way through the excited little mob and brazenly announcing himself as a physician knelt beside the motionless girl. A close look and a touch on wrist and heart, were enough to tell him the truth.

"Some one shut off that infernal light," he sharply commanded, "or steady it so I can see what has killed her. The Panther's Cub is dead."

In the long moment when the black dancer's lips clung to her throat they must have pressed home the tiny, deadly stiletto, its hilt a cork which he had held gripped between his teeth. What had looked no more than a caress in keeping with the spirit of their dance, was actually deliberate murder so skillfully executed that none of the many watching eyes, not even Traherne's own, had guessed the truth, or dreamed that seeming caress an actual death-kiss.

Inserted at the side of the throat, well behind the ear, the small sharp blade had penetrated back and upward into the base of the brain—the girl was probably already dead when the Panther laid her down and danced, light-footed, from the floor; to be lost past hope of immediate pursuit or capture in the depths of his infamous club.

Grimly Traherne pocketed the stiletto drawn from Mitza's throat—the manner in which a cork had been substituted for its original hilt so it could be more easily gripped by the Panther's teeth, might later serve as a clue, he reasoned, and if left where it was it would almost certainly be lost to the police.

Already the men in charge of the supper room were beginning to eye him suspiciously and the head waiter edged closer, perhaps bent on questioning him. Traherne decided the wisest course was to mix with the other patrons and let some one else notify the proper authorities. He drifted back toward his own table, listening while a stout, pompous man loudly told the head waiter what he ought to do. The stout gentleman wanted the coroner instantly summoned, the police notified, and the head waiter, evidently bent on delay, argued the point insisting that there was no need to spoil the evening because of an accident.

"Accident! It was deliberate murder!" the stout man spluttered, others took sides and under cover of the dispute over what should be done Traherne was able to slip quietly away, unnoticed except by an unimportant waiter or two who offered no interference.

Once on the street he looked right and left for any sign of Fisk or his men but they were too well hidden, the ill-lighted block appeared utterly deserted. He walked briskly to the first corner, turned it, then throwing caution to the winds, loudly whistled: "The Camels Are Coming."

Almost instantly a tall, wide-shouldered figure loomed up from no where in particular and Fisk's voice inquired if there was anything wrong.

"Everything!" Traherne bitterly retorted. "The Panther killed poor little Mitza and then danced gaily away."

"Killed her?" The inspector stopped short in his tracks.

"Yes, deliberately, under the eyes of the entire supper room—mine included! No." As Fisk swung on his heel, heading back toward the Panther's Den. "In the course of time somebody'll notify headquarters—and it's already too late for any hope of catching the Panther there—besides, there's something else we must do."

"Beg pardon, miss, is there anything I can get you, while Mr. Sanger is busy at the phone?" Daphne dragged reluctant eyes from the open square of the window at which she had been staring, lost in thought, while the soft-footed man servant hovered fussily about the room.

"No, nothing. Unless," as an afterthought, "you have some coffee?"

"Certainly, miss, in one little moment."

Did she imagine it, or was there an evilly suggestive smile lurking somewhere amid the correctly expressionless wrinkles of his weasoned face? Smiling or not, the stooping figure went back to its kitchen and next instant the foyer door opened to admit Murray Sanger wearing a gorgeously embroidered blue and orange Chinese lounging suit. He smiled at her, that charmingly whimsical smile of his that so completely atoned for any irregularities in the lean, gray eyed face.

"Satisfied? Though I suppose it's an old story—seeing your beauty beat down men's resistance—it must have more or less lost its thrill."

"You think it was only that? Because you resisted?"

"Well, as men go I'm not particularly attractive, and while, of course, I have more than average wealth I hardly think that much appealed to you."

"Has no woman ever told you that a strong personality, finely tempered, steel-sharp, means more to us than mere good looks, or even physical strength? But of course they have! You're only too well aware that the dominant male in you bends us, pliant as reeds, to your will."

"So far all the bending I've noticed has been on my side," he laughingly refused attunement to her more serious note. "It was you who insisted on coming here tonight—be honest, admit I did my damnedest to dissuade you."

"And you call that gallant? Reminding me that I had to fairly beg an invitation, or not really even that, only a grudging permission to talk with you alone."

"Now you're here, what is there to say?" his voice was suddenly somber, just for a second, then it lifted back to quizzical mockery. "Shall I tell you there was never a woman quite so beautiful—or that your hair is like loose flames circling your head and calling men's hands to caress it—or that your eyes— Hark, what was that?"

A scuffling sound and a small sharp crash had come from kitchenward. They listened, neither moving, until the unmistakable whining voice of his servant reached them in muffled apology:

"Sorry to delay, miss—one moment—I broke a cup."

"I had asked for coffee," Daphne explained. "But why so jumpy? Does entertaining a lady always jangle your nerves like that?"

"It might conceivably depend on the lady—but great suffering Caesar, hasn't there been enough to jangle them this past week? Not to mention today—with cemeteries, smashed funeral urns, and men who pop out of coffins! But of course you don't know what I'm talking about, you haven't heard how Myron and I played sleuth and—but I think that story can wait." He went a little closer to the chair in which she was sitting, to stand smiling down at her. "After all, my dear, being alone with you like this can't be described as precisely conducive to serene peace of mind. It's a bit risky, you know."

"For you or for me?"

He delayed answering because of the servant's entrance with coffee, but the gray eyes which for once failed to share in the smile of his lips, studied her intently as his servant arranged the coffee service on a table within easy reach.

"Your flowers are gorgeous," Daphne offered for sake of something to say while the man lingered at her elbow. She leant admiringly toward the banked rhododendrons filling the empty fireplace, one white finger stroking a velvet petal.

"I tried to match your hair, but it couldn't be done, they don't grow flowers that color." He, at least, had evidently not the slightest regard for what his servant might think of her midnight visit.

"Easier than to match bla—" The word stopped, bitten sharp off, for in turning from the hearth her glance had fallen on the cheek of the stooping servant still puttering over the coffee service, and it was smoothly firm, with not the sign of a wrinkle.

"Black hair, like Faith's." Sanger had mistaken the cause of that abrupt checking in mid-air. "But then, it takes a woman of flame and snow and jewel-bright yellow, to stir such fervor in a sluggish masculine brain."

Daphne let the speech go unanswered because she dared not quite trust her voice; before shuffling away the servant had turned to look full at her, and recognizing him she was able to guess the grim reason for that queer little scuffling sound they had heard in the kitchen.

"Coffee?" Her hands aimlessly played with the delicate china and Sanger, after a moment's watching, prisoned them both in his. Drawing her slowly to her feet.

"You could no more drink it than I could," he affirmed. "We've a different sort of thirst that cries for quenching! So—and so—and so—" his voice trailed off.

He was laughing again, between the fall of light kisses on temples, and cheeks, and throat, before his mouth fastened on hers. She felt herself lifted, crushed against him, and irresistibly borne toward the depths of a wide-pillowed couch—then he was half kneeling beside her, laughing down in a way that robbed his passion of all offence and made it no more than a feverish game that they played, together.

"Be serious," she begged. "Tell me what you meant just now, about cemeteries and coffins and men who pop out of them."

"No," he refused. "If you *will* visit men in the wee small hours, you mustn't expect them to sit, half a room away, telling of their latest adventures in pursuing escaped criminals and capturing dignified police inspectors instead." He chuckled at memory of the 'Hands up' scene in the Cardigan vault.

"You're saying just enough to make me wildly curious," she remonstrated. "And it isn't a bit fair—I told you it was the desire to talk over all the terrible things which have happened, that made me want to come here tonight."

"True, lady-dear, but in gaining your point you most willfully aroused another desire which has to be satisfied first. Did you honestly think me so cold I could sit, alone with your beauty, calmly talking of murders, clues, bungling police, and what should be done to straighten it all?"

"I thought—I still think—" It was never put into words for a bell shrilled sharply, someone pounded on the outer door.

"Now who the devil?" Sanger eyed her suspiciously. "Someone for you?"

"How could it be? I slipped out after the whole penthouse was quiet."

He moved, soft-footed, out into the apartment foyer and after a second Daphne followed him. As they reached the front door someone thumped on it and a voice called:

"Murray! I say, Murray! Are you there?"

"It's Myron! If he finds you here—"

"Well, what then? If you don't let him in he'll rouse the other tenants."

"Why not wait in the bed room? He won't stay long."

"Hiding's so stupid—it puts one hopelessly in the wrong. I'll go back to the living room and we'll carry on as if my being here were the most natural thing in the world."

"As you like."

When he had unfastened the door Myron burst in, a slightly cross and crumpled Whitney Page at his heels.

"Daphne's missing!" Myron ignored such formalities as a greeting or apology for disturbing his friend. "Faith woke in the night and wanted her, the nurse found she wasn't in her room so came to me. I hadn't gone to bed. We looked everywhere but I tell you she's gone! God knows what's happened to her!"

"Sorry you've been needlessly alarmed; she's here."

"Here!" Both men goggled at him as at someone gone suddenly mad.

"Why so astonished? Daphne came down to consult me about the best way of breaking news of her father's death to Faith."

It was a lame excuse but the best he could offer at such short notice and the others at least outwardly accepted it. All three went into the living room where Daphne was composedly smoking and sipping a cup of black coffee.

She had heard Sanger's statement of the reason for her visit so talked about Faith, and her hurt puzzlement over the continued nonappearance of her father, for whom she had repeatedly asked before finally settling to sleep.

Then Sanger and Myron between them told the other two of the mad chase to the Sleepy Hollow Cemetery and its dismal ending.

"We were all so startled when Fargo leaped up and shot through the door that none of us made a move to stop him—I think for a second we all believed he'd popped out of the coffin itself instead of up from behind it."

"But why should he want to go there? I don't under-stand."

"No more do we," Sanger told him. "After I'd seen Fargo peering out of a taxi window we simply trailed the cab and it led us past Tarrytown. When its passenger got out at the cemetery we parked my car and tried to follow him on foot, lost him in the darkness—suspected he might be headed for the Cardigan vault and after a lot of hunting found it just in time to hear its door click shut. Naturally we supposed it was Fargo who'd gone inside and only dis-covered the inspector's and Traherne's presence on the scene after Fargo had gotten clean away."

"Most inadequate police in the world," Whitney Page stated mournfully. "They should have caught the man before this."

"Oh well, New York's a bit large and he only bolted this morning," Sanger pointed out. "Ye gods but I'm popular tonight—there goes my doorbell again!"

He went to answer it, finding Inspector Fisk and Sydney Traherne in the outer hall.

"Hope we didn't root you out of bed," Fisk apologized, "but we'd no choice—one of my men reports seeing Fargo enter your apartment half an hour ago."

20

THE SINGLE BLOSSOM

"Come inside," Murray Sanger invited. "You'll find a regular gathering of the clans; Daphne Fane, Page, and Myron Stanwix. But you must be wrong about Fargo. Aside from my guests my servant and I have been alone in the apartment since I got back from the cemetery."

In the living room Sanger offered his latest guests coffee or a drink, both of which they refused. Myron rather haltingly tried to explain how the rest of them came to be in Murray Sanger's apartment at such an unholy hour ending:

"When I couldn't find Daphne, and could get no answer from Murray, though I was pretty well certain he must be in, I 'phoned Whitney Page and after he'd joined me we both came down here, thinking the door bell might wake him even if the telephone had failed."

Fisk's lips were open on a question when Sanger cut sharply in:

"You said nothing about trying to get me on the 'phone. What time was it?"

"Probably ten or fifteen minutes before I knocked on your door. Central said you didn't answer."

"But man, the phone didn't ring at all," Sanger protested. "We couldn't have missed hearing it."

He jumped up and made for the entrance foyer, returning a minute later carrying a telephone instrument from
which two feet or so of wire dangled helplessly.

"Wire cut—" his gray eyes had the cold brightness of
chilled steel. "Yet I used the instrument not half an hour
before you came." He set it down on a table and turned
toward Inspector Fisk. "Is Fargo the answer?"

"Hard to say. You spoke of your servant just now, where
is he, and why didn't he answer the doorbell?"

"I don't know. It seems he's scarcely had time to get
sound asleep since he brought in coffee. Let's investigate."

Telling the others to wait, he and Inspector Fisk went
through the entrance foyer into the small darkened kitch-
en, where Sanger cast an appraising eye over its ordered
neatness.

"Nothing wrong here. I suppose he simply thought I'd
want nothing more tonight and has gone to bed."

"Where does he sleep? It's as well to make sure."

"In a room at the end of this passage. Come, I'll show
you."

Sanger led the way to a closed door, paused a moment
outside it, then grasped the knob turning it so gently that
it made no sound and the door opened on a small, plainly
furnished room only lighted by a reading lamp that cast
a circle of brilliance down on the table and over an open
book just beneath it, while the man seated with his back
toward them was left in semi-gloom.

It was the man's ears that told Sanger it was not his
servant who sat there innocently absorbed in a book. The
stooping shoulders, familiar coat, even the slightly darker
hair might have passed muster in the dim light, but he
had been too often irritated by a pair of huge outstanding
ears that always looked as though they might flap in a too
strong breeze, not to instantly notice the neat pair fitting
close against this man's head.

Without a word he switched on the room's main light and sprang to seize the nearest shoulder, swinging the seated man around so they could see his face. It was Fargo, the vanished Stanwix butler.

"So it was you who cut my 'phone wire, and I suppose you're also responsible for the scuffling noise we heard in the kitchen—you were overpowering my servant."

"Yes." Fargo calmly assented, a somewhat cryptic smile decorating his handsome lips.

"But it was his voice that answered when I called."

"He'd an automatic against his temple and knew I'd shoot if he didn't obey me and reassure you."

"That was before the coffee was served." Sanger was rapidly thinking back and not liking his own thoughts. "It was you who brought that in?"

"Yes."

At the answer a certain grimness wiped the whimsical charm from Murray Sanger's face; he remembered Daphne's sudden start and her broken sentence—in that instant she must have recognized Fargo and yet said no word. Silently he cursed his own rapt absorption in a woman whom he now felt had all along been tricking him.

"Did you kill my servant? Where is he?"

"In there, safely trussed up." Fargo indicated the clothes closet where, in fact, they found the man tightly bound and gagged but otherwise unhurt.

When he had been released and stationed on guard in the entrance foyer, Fargo was taken to the living room and the others told what had happened.

"So you see, Mr. Sanger, my man wasn't wrong after all, about seeing Fargo enter your apartment." The inspector seemed openly delighted by the turn of events.

"Admitted, though I still can't guess why. Unless, perhaps, I was his next chosen victim."

"Well, the fact that the police caught him before he'd done more damage was due entirely to good luck, not good management," Whitney Page contributed with an undisguised sneer. "And he's so devilish calm about it that I'm beginning to worry for fear he knows they've not enough evidence to convict him."

"A little early though, now to talk about conviction, Mr. Page," Sydney Traherne drawled before his friend had time for a retort. "So far the inspector's said nothing at all about arresting Fargo—as a matter of fact I think he first intends going thoroughly over the case while the people most concerned happen, by such lucky chance, to be all gathered together."

There was a rapid, complex exchange of glances between the two, then Fisk nodded briefly and Traherne went on:

"When several murders have been committed, presumably by the same hand, it's generally best when considering them to take them up in the order in which they occurred. Suppose we begin with Peter Cardigan's murder, while the parade was passing his windows.

"We know he had previously quarreled with his closest friend, Mark Stanwix, also that at lunch that day he received a communication in the shape of a sketch, or drawing, which greatly upset him, and that he had told Letty, the cleaning woman, to stay out of his office as he expected a visitor.

"Now, between the time when he returned to the office after lunch and the time of his death, we know he repeatedly tried to get in touch with his son; the fact that he 'phoned several times both to his own apartment and to the Stanwix penthouse being vouched for by the Cardigans' maid and the Stanwix butler. Therefore I think we may reasonably conclude that he knew himself threatened by a danger in some way connected with the drawing sent him by mail, and that he was anxious to make some important communication to Kent before the arrival of the visitor whom we know he expected.

"Failing to reach his son by 'phone he wrote him a letter which the murderer afterwards found and burned. What it contained we shall probably never know—unless Fargo who, the cleaning woman swears, visited Peter Cardigan's office that afternoon, is able and willing to enlighten us."

Thus indirectly appealed to, the butler's handsome face became a study of indecision, his very uncertainty betraying the fact that the secret of that burned letter was known to him, though he evidently much doubted the wisdom of revealing it.

"Surely we've reached the time for plain speaking," Traherne encouraged him. "Perhaps it will help you to decide if I mention finding a few particles of cocaine adhering to a scrap of paper near the smashed funeral urns in the Cardigans' family vault. Everyone here tonight already knows the real nature of Peter Cardigan's business."

"Then—" Fargo still hesitated, his questioning eyes rapidly fleeing from one intent face to another. Something read in one of them gave him a cue to frankness. "Then, I shall need to explain that during the four months I held the position of butler in the Stanwix penthouse, Mr. Cardigan showed me an unusual kindness and consideration," he began. "So much so that I grew to like him and when his voice came over the wire on Saturday, filled with an unmistakable terror I couldn't help becoming anxious as to what was wrong with him, and a little later stopping at his office to ask if there was anything I could do."

"One moment," Traherne quietly interrupted. "I suppose it was really you whom Letty saw entering the office?"

"Yes."

"But she particularly mentioned a gray suit that caught her fancy,—why weren't you in uniform at that hour?"

"Because I'd been out on a personal errand and went direct to Mr. Cardigan's office before returning to the penthouse."

"Thanks, the point seemed a bit confusing. Please go on."

"The hall door was unlocked and the outer office deserted, but when I knocked on the door marked private Mr. Cardigan first called out to know who was there and then let me in. I think he was glad to see me, and in a state of terror that almost necessitated confiding in someone. At any rate, after first swearing me to secrecy, he told how, years ago, he became involved in serious financial difficulties and was facing actual ruin when a friend came to his rescue by offering him a share in his own illicit, but extremely lucrative business—the wholesale importing and distributing of various drugs.

"At the time I guessed the unnamed friend to be Mark Stanwix, though later events seem to prove the idea a mistake. Be that as it may, Mr. Cardigan went on to explain that he had recently come into serious conflict with a certain—also unnamed—member of their organization who was utterly ruthless and without the rudiments of a moral sense.

"He was quite evidently terrified of this man whom he considered an enemy, but of course under the circumstances there was no one to whom he could apply for protection against him without risking betrayal of his own disgraceful traffic in smuggled drugs. When it was too late I realized Mr. Cardigan must have had an appointment with the man for that afternoon, but for some reason he failed to mention the fact; only asking me to take charge of a letter he had just written to his son, so that in case anything happened Kent would know the name of his father's enemy and be able to exact vengeance.

"If he'd only given me the letter, then, the whole course of events might have been altered, but at the last moment he changed his mind saying he had thought of something which must be added to the already written letter and promising to bring it up to the penthouse as soon as he had made the necessary addition.

"Perhaps he didn't altogether trust me, or perhaps he so hated the idea of letting Kent know about the drug business that he couldn't quite bear to let his own written confession out of his hands. Wanting to keep it where it could be instantly destroyed in case he decided against letting his son ever know the truth. Whatever his motive, he put the letter back under the blotter on his desk and asked me to leave him, he felt a need of being alone.

"In face of his declared wish for solitude I could hardly insist on staying, but all the rest of that day and all Sunday I worried about him, and when Inspector Fisk and Sydney Traherne came to the penthouse the next evening, asking to see Kent Cardigan, I instantly guessed that the worst had happened."

"Thanks for giving us an idea what the burned letter contained," Traherne spoke as soon as he saw that Fargo had finished.

"Faugh! You surely don't mean taking such a flimsy tissue of lies seriously?" Whitney Page almost snorted his disgust, "It's clearly only made up to clear his own skirts of Peter Cardigan's murder!"

"So?" Traherne paid his outburst only the scantest attention, his thoughts quite obviously busy with something else. "This letter evidently gave no clue as to the hiding place of a huge quantity of drugs which Mr. Cardigan had secreted somewhere," he appeared to be thinking aloud, "yet it must have mentioned this secret store judging by the search afterwards conducted by his murderer. Perhaps the fact that such a store existed was already known to his enemy?

"At least we may feel certain of one fact, the letter said nothing of the secret's being contained in Peter Cardigan's safety deposit box, for once the importance attached to that box became generally known the murderer stopped searching elsewhere and concentrated on it.

"We've all along surmised that the guilty person was conversant with most of what happened in the Stanwix penthouse—either possessing personal access or having placed a spy there, so it's not astonishing that Mark Stanwix' intention of handing the key over to Kent at midnight on Tuesday leaked out, hard as we tried to prevent its doing so.

"I wasn't present when Kent Cardigan died, but later on was told Inspector Fisk's reasons for believing no one in the room with him guilty of his murder. You're all more or less familiar with those reasons, but it will do no harm to go over them again.

"First as to motive. It was assumed that Kent was stabbed to prevent his opening his father's safety deposit box, not because of a desire to gain possession of the key itself, since it was afterwards found on the floor not far from where Kent had been standing.

"The knife with which he was stabbed was missing, while a frazzle of silk on the window catch, a silk cord carelessly dropped near a flower bed in which someone appeared to have recently cleaned a knife, and a rope ladder dangling over the edge of the roof, all suggested a murderer lurking outside the house. A murderer, who, when the lights went out, hurled a dagger through the open window striking Kent's heart, then pulled it outside again by means of a silk cord attached to the hilt and after, for some unexplained reason, stopping to clean his knife in the flower bed, escaped by way of the rope ladder.

"Hearing of all these various clews in what might be called cold blood, long after their discovery, they struck me as a trifle obvious. Very nicely arranged, of course, if designed to clear those in the study from all suspicion, but stupid if real—and our murderer was certainly not that, whatever else he might be.

"Once a doubt of the genuineness of those outside clews found foothold in my mind I naturally looked for evidence confirming my belief that Kent Cardigan had been stabbed not by someone lurking outside the window, but by one of the people who were with him in the study when its lights were extinguished.

"The most telling argument against that theory was the absence of the weapon used, but on the other hand I gathered that none of those present had been searched; because the clues pointing to an outside agency turned up before proceedings had reached that stage. Therefore it was possible that the murderer had simply concealed the knife somewhere in his clothing, being quite aware that the dropped rope, disturbed flower bed and hanging ladder would be found in time to prevent a personal search of those inside the study.

"Yet that explanation though plausible wasn't satisfactory—it entailed too great a risk. The smallest hitch as to time, or impetuosity on Fisk's part might easily have led to an immediate personal search and discovery of the concealed weapon. I entertained too much respect for our murderer's intelligence to believe he'd disposed of the death-weapon in that way, but if not—how else?

"He couldn't have flung it out the window, for it wasn't found on the roof and the edge of the building was too far away for it to have fallen over into the street; he could have scarcely taken it away with him. There remained the alternative that it must be still hidden somewhere in the study.

"But where? The room had been searched, though only by artificial light, and a dagger long enough to strike deep into a man's heart isn't a thing to escape notice from trained searchers, particularly when the person hiding it has only a limited time at his disposal. I was still puzzling over a solution of the problem when the strengthening morning light struck on a pot of flowering tulips and their brilliant color caught, and held, my eyes.

"Not that I for a second suspected any sinister reason for their presence, I was simply half absently admiring the contrast between the vivid yellow flowers and their glossy green leaves, when an errant breeze blew in through the open window and I noticed a strange peculiarity about one of the plants—all the rest gently bent to the touch of the wind but this one remained stiffly erect.

"Then a careful touch of my fingertip told me the unbending flower and its two guardian leaves were wrought of metal. They had nothing but outward appearance in common with the other plants which they so perfectly matched.

"Inspector Fisk will doubtless blame me for not at once confiding in him, but by that time I strongly suspected our murderer's identity, though I hadn't a scrap of evidence to back my belief, and feared that if I passed on such few disconnected facts as I possessed he would either take alarm and escape before we could gather enough evidence to justify his arrest, or else indulge in some more killings—quite possibly of Inspector Fisk himself if he once realized him as a dangerous antagonist.

"Wisely or not, I kept silent and took the pot of tulips away with me. Later examination proved my supposition correct; the two wide leaves and the single blossom that declined bending to the breeze formed the skillfully wrought hilt of a dagger the blade of which was sunk into the earth in which the other plants were innocently rooted."

21
THE OTHER THREE

To realize the full effect of Sydney Traherne's revelation it must be remembered that of those present, or close to the study at the time of Kent Cardigan's murder, only Mark Stanwix and Faith were absent from the group he addressed. What he said was tantamount to an accusation from which only he, himself and Inspector Fisk might feel themselves completely free.

In the study at the moment it was plunged in darkness were Mark Stanwix, his son, Whitney Page, Murray Sanger, Fisk and Kent Cardigan. Of those six men two were dead, and Inspector Fisk automatically exempt from suspicion; remained, Whitney Page, Murray Sanger, and Myron Stanwix.

To further complicate matters Fargo had spoken near the door which no one remembered to have heard open, while the study was still dark, and Daphne Fane acknowledged being somewhere just outside that same door during at least some of those few critical minutes. It would have been physically possible for either of them to have committed the murder and still reached the given points in the time available.

Of the seven people in Murray Sanger's living room any one of five might conceivably be guilty—Fisk and Traherne being the only two outside the circle of possible suspects.

Not a pleasant situation. It was hardly surprising that faces reddened or paled according to their owner's reaction to temperamental disturbance, or that eyes peered suspiciously, locked with other eyes, and then shifted as if ashamed of their own readiness to doubt even close friends.

Their host attempted to relieve the tension by declaring that drinks all around were strongly indicated but the suggestion fell flat, they were all too intent on Sydney Traherne's next words.

"Going back to the question of motive," he resumed, "I think Kent Cardigan was killed not only to prevent his using the safety deposit key that night, but also to enable the murderer to open the box himself. He couldn't actually steal the key, its disappearance would have nullified all those carefully arranged clews pointing to an outside agency, but you'll remember the lights were timed to go out at the exact instant when Kent held the key in his hand, so that after stabbing him his assailant need waste no precious seconds in searching his pockets, he had only to take the key from Kent's fingers as death relaxed them.

"Working quickly under cover of the darkness, an impression was taken in wax brought along already prepared and the key itself dropped not far from Kent's body. In confirmation of that theory Inspector Fisk will tell you I found a few flakes of wax on the carpet close to where the key had lain."

"One moment, Mr. Traherne." Whitney Page had completely altered his manner; he was now the benign, silky voiced little fop whom opponents in the law courts knew, and secretly dreaded. "If, as you say, the murderer became possessed on Tuesday night of an impression from which a duplicate key could be made, why was it not used at some time on Wednesday? Why was it necessary to wait until Thursday, by which time it became compulsory to slay Mark Stanwix in order to prevent his first opening the box?"

"Sorry, Page, but not being the murderer I'm unable to say precisely what went on inside his head, though it strikes me as probable that he hardly dared use the key on Wednesday fearing the police might have guessed at the wax impression taken and set a watch in the safety deposit vaults. He doubtless thought it wiser to wait a few days, watching developments and making sure the coast was clear. Then Mark Stanwix' sudden decision to open the box himself on Thursday afternoon upset his calculations and forced an alteration in his plans. Which, by the way, brings up the question: how many people knew of Mr. Stanwix' decision?"

"Has it occurred to you that among all those unfortunate enough to lie under the shadow of possible suspicion the charming lady in our midst," Whitney Page bowed to her with a slightly exaggerated homage, "is the one who all along possessed the best opportunity for knowing exactly what went on, and what was planned, in the Stanwix penthouse? If you will cast your mind back over the sad and lurid events of this tragic week, you may recall that she was even present, though presumably asleep, when Mark Stanwix announced his intention of giving Kent his father's safety deposit key at the first instant such a course became strictly legal; in other words at midnight on Tuesday last."

"As it happens, this is the first I've heard of Miss Fane's being present that night," Traherne answered. "You've doubtless forgotten I wasn't there myself. You and Inspector Fisk were alone with Mr. Stanwix."

"Quite true," Page conceded after an instant's reflection. "I have become so accustomed to seeing you and Fisk always together that I failed to remember your absence on that particular occasion. Still, that absence in no way affects the point at issue—Miss Fane's omnipresence throughout the case."

Daphne's golden-yellow eyes regarded the dapper little lawyer with half sleepy, half amused contempt.

"Are you trying to accuse me of committing an atrocious series of murders, Mr. Page?"

"Not at all," he reprovingly contradicted. "I merely wish to point out a few facts illustrative of your, shall we say suspicious behavior, and your possible complicity with the man known to us under the name of the Panther."

"You'd be simply wasting time," Traherne cut in before Page could go on. "Daphne Fane is a highly valued member of the United States Secret Service, and has all along been following the trail of the Panther."

"What?" the amazed ejaculation came from Inspector Fisk. "Is that the truth?"

"Absolutely—though I only recently learned the facts. Perhaps you'll be good enough to explain a few of them, Miss Fane?"

"If I must," she agreed with obvious reluctance. "You see, this case didn't actually begin with the murder of Peter Cardigan, it goes back some eight or ten years, possibly even longer. During all that time the narcotic agents have suspected a wealthy and most efficiently organized ring of drug importers and distributers here in New York, but while they sometimes succeeded in catching some of its smaller fry they were never able to discover the identity of the man, or men, at its head. Certain indications pointed to a single leader, but there was no certainty, and of course drugs come under the narcotic laws and are seldom or never touched by the Secret Service unless, as in this instance, they branch out into some other line.

"About two years ago rumors concerning a mysterious individual known as the Panther began floating about, and it gradually became known that he didn't confine his activities to drugs. Such things as bank robberies, jewels, and even blackmail also interested him.

"It was in connection with the latter that I entered the case. This Panther had in some way got hold of certain secret papers belonging to one of the Embassies in Washington, and was using them for the purpose of blackmail. Diplomatic reasons forbade an appeal to the police so the embassy confided its troubles, or a part of them, to our Government. As a result I was sent to New York with orders to find the Panther.

"Forgive me, Myron," she flung him a sweetly apologetic smile, "but certain evidence indicated that either your father or Peter Cardigan was actually the Panther, with the balance of probability favoring the former. My visit to the Connecticut house party was arranged through its host, a man in the confidence of certain high government officials, for the express purpose of making friends with your sister and gaining an entry into your home. You know I succeeded but perhaps you don't realize that my presence there very nearly cost Faith her life; it was for my benefit that Tibits' claws were poisoned. They feared I knew too much and wanted me permanently retired from the picture."

"But Tibits was my sister's pet, not yours," Myron objected.

"True, still he'd taken a decided fancy to me and, if you remember, it was I who first went to the window in answer to his cries. At the moment he was freed I was leaning from it so that anyone outside could easily see and identify me."

"Please observe how every smallest item proves the Panther's intimate knowledge of what went on in the penthouse," Whitney Page requested. "Surely a knowledge closer than that of any mere guest or friend—in short, one is well-nigh driven into concluding him an inmate." He paused, looking directly at Inspector Fisk. "All things considered I am at a loss to understand why we continue conversing and explaining. Surely Fargo's guilt is so obvious that instantly arresting him is the only rational course of procedure."

"Unluckily arrest is the first step toward a trial and a jury," Fisk pointed out. "When I've no real evidence against him and am not myself convinced of his guilt, how the devil can I hope to convince a jury?"

Page eyed him with the air of one who determinedly clings to his patience against almost overwhelming odds. Then he pulled a chair forward and sat down, his plump knees wide apart, his even plumper hands dangling between them.

"After all we mustn't forget that these horrible murders are entirely different from the type of crime filling our daily papers," he began. "All three took place inside the one building, and there appears to be no question of an ordinary criminal being in any way concerned. The murderer must undoubtedly possess an intimate knowledge of the private lives and plans of his victims. Now, as I see it, only two persons possessed both such knowledge and the opportunity to act upon it. Miss Fane and Fargo. Since her connection with the Secret Service automatically eliminates Miss Fane we are left with one possible suspect— Fargo."

"What's wrong with the other three of you?" Traherne gently inquired, between puffs of his cigarette.

"Three?" The little lawyer abruptly bounced around in his chair to glare at the speaker. "Three? What might you be trying to insinuate?"

"Only that Murray Sanger, Myron Stanwix and you, yourself possessed equal knowledge and equal opportunity. In fact, if we put Fargo temporarily on one side, it seems that one of you three must be guilty. For of course you're perfectly right in saying the Panther's no ordinary member of the underworld."

22
THANKS TO THE WOMAN

"Alibis! There happens to be such a thing as an alibi!" The little lawyer's firmly held patience snapped under pressure of his own inclusion among Sydney Traherne's three suspects. "I, for one, was nowhere near any of the victims, save Kent Cardigan, at the time of their death."

"So say we all," Traherne answered with a somewhat enigmatic smile. "Suppose we trot out these various alibis and have a look at them in cold blood. Take your own, for example; you say at the moment Peter Cardigan was killed you were at a picture show—alone. You were admittedly close to Kent Cardigan at the instant he was stabbed. You were the very last person seen with Mark Stanwix before his death, leaving the penthouse dining room with him and next appearing in the bank—alone. What price alibis now?"

"Why—why—it's perfectly outrageous!" Whitney Page fairly spluttered with wrath. "I was never accused of such a thing in my life!"

"No. As a general thing one isn't apt to be more than once in a lifetime. But as it happens I'm not accusing you; only pointing out that you haven't the ghost of a decent alibi to bless yourself with. Now in that respect Mr. Sanger is in much better case. Thanks to the all-seeing news reel camera we know the bank clock on the Stanwix

building pointed to the exact hour of three as the death-
noose closed about Peter Cardigan's throat: at which time
he claims to have been descending in one of the elevators
on the opposite side of the building. His statement is cor-
roborated by the boy, Paddy, and by another quite disin-
terested passenger.

"Of course he was in the study with all the rest of
you when Kent Cardigan died, but on the other hand Myron Stanwix vouches for his being in the Bronx at the
time of the murder in the private elevator. Considering
all of which facts I feel sure you'll admit he's much better
equipped as regards alibis than you yourself."

"Outrageous! Perfectly outrageous!" Page was beyond
the power of coherent speech. Traherne merely grinned at
him and went calmly on.

"And then if we take up Myron Stanwix; his position
seems nicely balanced between yours and Mr. Sanger's. His
story of searching Fifth Avenue for ties of a certain shade
remains unsupported; you've none of you any for the time
in the darkened study; and for this afternoon when his father was killed, we have Murray Sanger's word that he was
in the Bronx so there he scores one over you. But—" Traherne paused to light another cigarette, "the inspector will
tell you that alibis are tricky things, even the best of them.

"For example take this afternoon's hunt for a real or
imagined Fargo. I've been thinking it over and made a few
notes as to time." He took a piece of paper from his pocket
and consulted it now and then as he went on: "When questioned in the bank you both told Inspector Fisk that after
seeing the man you thought was Fargo you parked Sanger's
car at approximately 1:10 and immediately went into the
department store which you thought you'd seen Fargo
enter. A few minutes later, say at 1:15 you were separated
by the crowd and as a matter of cold fact neither of you
saw the other again for more than an hour.

"According to your story you both searched about the department store, unsuccessfully hunting one another for some little time, and afterwards made a couple of trips to the parked car, but separately, not both happening to return to it at the same time, so that you failed to meet until about quarter to three.

"Now, from 1:15 to, say, 2:45 gives us an hour and thirty minutes during which time either one of you, instead of aimlessly drifting about the Bronx, could have rushed downtown by subway, crossed to the Stanwix Building, gone up to the twentieth floor—where the hole in the storage room wall was already prepared—shot Mr. Stanwix as he went down to keep his appointment at the bank, then descended to the street again, entered the safety deposit vaults before his murder was discovered or any alarm raised, used the key made from the wax impression to open Peter Cardigan's box, still before the alarm had spread outside the private office—rushed uptown by subway and innocently met the other at Sanger's parked car.

"Admittedly there would have been no time to spare, still with any sort of luck it could have been managed, and of course, since I find you both rent private boxes in the Stanwix Bank Vaults, you'd have attracted no attention from the men on guard there. Knowing you well by sight and name your entrance today would have simply left no impression on their minds."

"Myron, old dear, it begins to look as if you were in for trouble," Murray Sanger observed with a half quizzical glance at his friend. "*Why* didn't you pick a row with one of those salespeople, or steal a tie, or any old thing to fix yourself in the shop people's memory? You can see Mr. Traherne has no earthly respect for anybody's unsupported word."

Without giving Myron time to answer had he been so minded, Traherne leaned a little forward, lids dropping over his singular eyes so that it was impossible to tell exactly whom he was watching, and went calmly on:

"So far we've been dealing only with the three murders of which you all know—tonight saw a fourth, perhaps the rottenest of all added to the tragic list."

There was a shocked cry from Daphne, a muttered word or ejaculation from all of the men but Inspector Fisk.

"Not—not Faith?" Daphne was already half out of her chair, bent on rushing to the sick girl whom she had left upstairs.

"No," Traherne reassured her, "not Faith." Then: "All of you except Whitney Page admittedly know a little concerning the night club called The Panther's Den, but my own personal knowledge goes a bit deeper. If you've the patience I'd like telling you my experiences there."

He briefly sketched how his own and the inspector's interest in the club was first roused by Kent Cardigan's going there on the very night his father's murder was discovered, and stimulated by Fargo's visit and subsequent disappearance, that same night, into the room holding the telephone booths. Then went on to tell of his own return the following evening, his successful penetration into the Den's most private regions and the weird scene where the voice of the unseen Panther spoke to his followers from behind the grill in the wall.

"Perhaps our reasons for connecting this mysterious night club owner with the murder of Peter Cardigan were a bit sketchy at first," he acknowledged, "but as I tell you every incident of that scene in the bare upper room was firmly etched in my memory. When I discovered that the dagger used to stab Kent Cardigan had a hilt made to resemble a solitary tulip blossom and its two guardian leaves, I knew that wasn't the first time that particular yellow color had been thrust on my notice within the last few days. I'd seen a silk square of that identical color given to the Panther's man, Andre, whom I afterwards learned to be a clever worker in metals.

"The pot of tulips bought by Daphne Fane had been in the study for some few days. Quite obviously the Panther stole a yellow petal, matched it with a bit of silk, and gave the latter to Andre as a color sample for the hilt of the dagger he was to make for the already planned murder in the study. After that 'Panther' and 'Murderer' became interchangeable terms—there was no doubting their linked identity.

"Leaving him for the moment I'll pass on to the girl known as the Panther's Cub whom Kent Cardigan loved. Incidentally I've no doubt it was she who failed to keep the Saturday luncheon appointment with him at Schrafft's; an appointment probably made at the Panther's instigation to assure Kent's absence from the Stanwix Building at the time it was planned to kill his father."

"I have told you how this girl hid me when the Panther's pack were in full cry at my heels, and how at my next vis-it she showed a faint tendency to talk of the Panther. He must have in some way learned that she was no longer to be implicitly trusted, so tonight he took the place of her ordinary partners and near the close of their dance, when he held her in his arms, apparently half swooning with love, kissed her throat.

"A death kiss that thrust a tiny stiletto into the base of her brain and forever robbed her of the power to betray him. Now—" Traherne's tone suddenly altered, grew crisp-ly incisive, "when the Panther danced tonight he wore a glove-like suit of satin, a costume that to preserve its sym-metry would permit of his wearing little or nothing under it, and also one that could hardly be discarded at a sec-ond's notice because it was made all in one piece, and, as I say, fitted tight as a glove.

"After he laid Mitza down and danced off the floor he had no means of knowing how soon the alarm would be raised, nor how far it would spread. His one idea must have been to get away from the night club as quickly as possible—away to some safe refuge where he could change at his leisure.

"Believing we knew his identity, and that he would make straight for the Stanwix Building, Inspector Fisk and I raced here; to find that everybody closely connected with the case had obligingly congregated here in Sanger's apartment. One of you is still wearing the Panther's dance-suit—there hasn't been time to change."

"Fargo! Of course it's Fargo." Whitney Page bounced from his chair and pointed an accusing finger at the tranquilly seated butler. "That's why he stole the uniform-coat belonging to Murray's servant; so its high collar would hide the absence of linen!"

"No harm to take a look." Traherne rose with a complete lack of haste and sauntered toward Fargo who awaited his coming without the movement of a muscle. Whitney Page, on the other hand, bobbed frantically about like a distracted hen, while Myron, Sanger, and Daphne remained perfectly motionless, all their eyes intent on Traherne.

Halfway across the room, without any preliminary slackening of his leisurely pace, he swerved suddenly to the left and in the same instant Murray Sanger's chair crashed over backward as he gained his feet with one lithe spring and a single, curt, commanding cry.

"Fargo!"

Fargo's answering leap bridged the distance—all three men locked in a struggle, violent, but so brief it gave time for no interference from the others. In the surprise of finding the man for whose help he had called against him, Sanger's resistance lacked coordination, he was overpowered, an arm imprisoned by either man, and the gorgeous Chinese lounging suit ripped open across the breast displaying the smooth-fitting black of the Panther's dance costume beneath it.

"Traitor!" His gray eyes blazed at Fargo with an infinite scorn.

"No," the other quietly denied. "Quite true to my salt. I've been more than six months on the trail of the Panther and only joined the Den's crew of assorted cutthroats in the hope of uncovering his real identity." He hesitated a split second, then added: "It was through my reports and advice that Daphne Fane was assigned to the case."

"Really?" Not once had Sanger looked at the woman, but his voice held an odd note as it framed a question. "What is she to you?"

"A highly valued colleague in the Service and—my wife."

"So." Sanger's manner suddenly lost its suggestion of controlled savagery—he was again the whimsical, gayly cynical person so familiar to all of them. "No need of hanging onto my arms like a couple of rampant bulldogs," he remarked, the pointed eyebrows climbing in unison with the smile suddenly softening the grim line of his lips. "I could do with a cigarette and after all I'm fairly caught—thanks to the woman."

23

ANY WEAPONS

At a sign from Traherne, Fargo let go the arm he held and once free of both men Sanger refastened the silk loops of his Chinese coat, then perched on the edge of a table, helping himself to a cigarette from the nearest silver box.

"Singular, how despite all warning and experience even clever men *will* continue walking blindly into traps baited with a morsel of smooth, white flesh."

He was eyeing them without a trace of animosity— quite his normal, lovable self, and not one of them found it entirely easy to realize him as the dreaded Panther, who for days past had been looming, a terrifying menace, in the background of their thoughts.

"For make no mistake, it was the woman who got me— not you." He grinned at Traherne. "At first I distrusted her, felt she was more than likely a spy. When she so glibly furnished the Panther Den's precise name and location I was practically certain she'd be better dispensed with so I poisoned Tibits' claws. But, to my own undoing, I weakened, pulled her aside when the cat had all but reached her arms. You see she'd got into my blood. No other woman had really mattered, even with Faith it was her father's money more than the girl herself. I knew, spy or not I had to have her—had to keep tonight's appointment and either win her consent to fleeing with me or else take her away by force.

"I knew the game was up, I'd attracted too much attention, a new start elsewhere was strongly indicated and if it hadn't been for Daphne I'd have left for parts unknown the instant I got possession of the fortune in drugs Peter Cardigan stole from my father, and from me."

"Your father?" Myron and Whitney Page simultaneously echoed on a note of sheer amazement.

"Oh yes," Sanger carelessly assured them. "It was he who invented and organized the racket years ago when I was only a kid. Myron can tell you I thought the sun rose and set in my dad; when I was twenty he gradually initiated me into the game he and Peter Cardigan played, and after he died I carried on."

What tragedy of a boy's blind hero-worship and the consequent warping of a nature, lay behind the simple statement?

"It wasn't until lately I discovered Cardigan senior had been systematically robbing both my dad and me for years. Of each drug consignment that passed through his hands some stuck fast to his fingers and was stored away against the day when he meant to retire and live a sweetly respectable life on the proceeds.

"We were both natural spendthrifts, dad and I, and besides, our racket was expensive. We'd saved so little that when I knew real trouble from Washington was headed my way, I hadn't enough for a comfortable start in some other clime—and I'd no intention of roughing it. So I issued fair warning, either Peter Cardigan disgorged that hidden store or he died.

"Well, he didn't quite believe I meant it, and after I'd proved myself a man of my word I couldn't find the drugs. It was you who furnished my first clew, Mr. Traherne, by mentioning this safety deposit box of Peter Cardigan's."

"Yes." Traherne nodded. "I did that to see if you'd bite."

"So you suspected me that early. Why?"

"Too perfect a three o'clock alibi—I wondered if you hadn't known in advance one was going to be needed."

"You discovered how it was worked?"

"Not till yesterday. Then, when fairly cornered, the bank employee in charge of the clock confessed accepting a bribe to hold the clock back seven minutes on Saturday last. In that way you were able to establish your presence in the descending elevator at the real hour of three, and still make Peter Cardigan's office when the clock under his window pointed to that precise time."

"I'd a hunch you were casting an inquisitive eye my way, but I had to stick it till I'd got hold of that fortune in drugs. Also, though I guessed Daphne as dangerous she's a most talented artist and half convinced me at least her love was real. I suppose all along she was actually following instructions, Traherne, even when she fooled me into letting her come here tonight."

"As to that, yes," Traherne acknowledged, "and a nice shock I got when you danced as the Panther. If you were here with Daphne, as planned, how could you also be at the Den? For a little I thought my theories smashed and that I'd picked the wrong man."

"Only a question of close shaving the time. My man let her in, said I was busy at the 'phone, and puttered about until he heard me moving in my room. Unfortunately I only took time to slip on a lounging suit high collared enough to hide the Panther's costume. Shows how disaster follows on too great haste. But even at that I might have made a clean get-away if Fargo had been my man as I thought. If he's in the S.S. why did he bolt this morning?"

"Because if arrested he'd have been forced either into inaction, or into telling who he was, and feared if he did the latter you'd somehow get to know and clear out before our case was complete. I say 'our' but up to today we've been working separately, not together."

"That's what fooled me, I think." Sanger nodded with a certain impersonal interest. "I could never catch the sign of an understanding. Also, while I've prided myself on the ability to read people, I'd have sworn Inspector Fisk sincerely liked me."

"He did," Traherne retorted. "And realizing how that same genuine liking was apt to throw you off guard, I took pains never to weaken it. If Fisk has a professional fault it's that he's too honest; those blue eyes of his could never have held quite such frank liking if he'd once thought of you in the Panther's role—one of the big reasons I didn't confide in him. The other two being fear of endangering his life, and of warning you."

"Since we're favoring stud-poker, with most of our cards face up, why not tell me what brought you and Daphne to partnership?"

"It was a footprint," Traherne enlightened him. "When Fargo bolted and we searched the penthouse for him Daphne was in her own room, serenely brushing her hair. Of course she denied seeing Fargo, but the door to her private bath was wide open and on the soft bathmat I saw the print of a man's shoe; all things considered it wasn't difficult to guess the butler had sought refuge with her and was even then hiding inside the circle of the casually arranged shower-bath curtain.

"None of the rest had my reasons for doubting the lady, so accepted her word that bedroom and bath were empty of other occupants than herself. While they searched elsewhere I went back to show Daphne the print on the bathmat and demand an accounting. After which we three worked together."

"And Fargo's trip to the Cardigan vault?"

"You must realize things have worked pretty rapidly these last few hours, and in the general rush Fargo and I slipped a cog. We'd arranged for him to leave the Stanwix building, disguised, of course, after the heat of the chase had somewhat cooled. He was to go to the Panther's Den and wait there until I later on kept my tentative appointment with Mitza.

"Meanwhile, not daring to disappear long enough for a personal raid on the Cardigan vault and unwilling, I think, to trust such a huge fortune in the hands of any one man, you selected three of your most trusted tools for the job and a little later Fargo got wind of what was happening. He tried to reach me, failed, so made a stab at saving the stuff alone; arrived too late and was surprised inside the vault by Fisk and myself.

"Then you and Myron turned up before he'd decided whether to declare himself while the inspector was with me and he felt he'd be more useful outside than in. He came back to keep an eye on the Panther's Den, saw me leave it and meet Fisk and this time decided we'd better join forces. We sent him on ahead to silence your man servant and see that no harm befell Daphne—for Mitza's fate taught us that a woman's life meant no more to you than a man's."

"Why should it? I've found them a treacherous lot. One came here today, saw the place full of flowers and guessed they were to welcome some other woman. She left a note threatening to tell everything she knew unless I promised undivided devotion. Thereby she signed her own death warrant. While as for the other—well, to me the man who kills quickly, painlessly, no matter for what reason, is less contemptible than the huntress who baits the death-trap with her body's beauty and the caress of her lying lips. She's not playing the game."

His eyes sought Daphne's for the first time since he and
Traherne had begun to talk, then he left his perch on the
table to lounge nearer to where she sat.

"It's fair to use *any* weapons against a killer and thief,"
Daphne told him. "Where are the drugs you stole from the
Cardigan vault?"

"Sad to say they're reposing in my safe at the Den; no
harm telling you as of course Fisk will round up my gang
and close the place, but—" and standing beside her chair
he laughed mockingly down into Daphne's beautiful upturned face, "why accuse me of stealing them? I was doing
no more than take back my own."

She was sitting somewhat apart from the others, so that
when Sanger smoothly bent just a little closer and, still
laughing, caught her chin in one hand, the nape of her neck
in the other, no one was near enough to interfere. Traherne
knew that grip for a jiu-jitsu hold, knew that in another
second Daphne's neck would be sharply broken by one
skilled snap—and there was no time in which to reach her!

He caught up a silver cigarette box from the table and
hurled it at Sanger. The box caught him on the elbow and
Sanger's arm dropped helpless for just the heartbeat or two
that gave Fargo and Fisk time to close in on him.

Beaten, he offered no resistance, not even when the
inspector's men came in and rather roughly snapped handcuffs on his wrists.

"Strong arm stuff unnecessary. I've sense enough to
know when the game is up," he said. Then he turned to
Daphne, that whimsical smile still on his lips. "Farewell,
dear Lady-Judas, let your kisses go on betraying men to
their destruction. At least I believe you won't soon forget
that your lips have twice been prey of the Panther."

He went tranquilly out between his captors, the shining
handcuffs gleaming on his wrists,—a laugh that was mock-
ing, contemptuous, and yet held real if sardonic mirth,
floating back to those whom he left in the room.

The Hollow Tree Mystery

MADELON ST. DENIS

The Jekyll-Hyde Murder Case

MADELON ST. DENIS

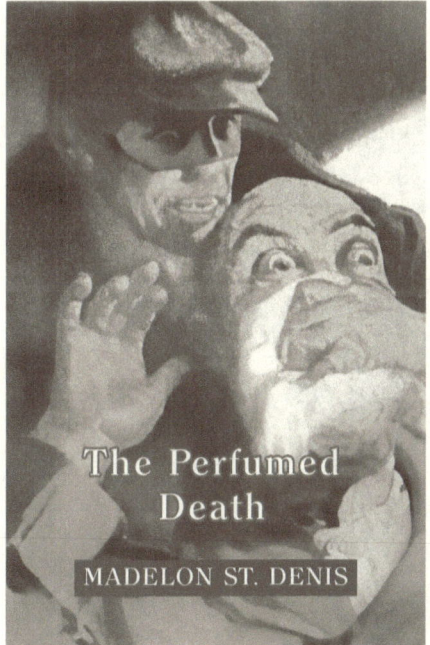

The Perfumed Death

MADELON ST. DENIS

The MURDERS AT HILLSIDE

VIRGINIA RATH

Coachwhip Publications
CoachwhipBooks.com

DEATH
ON THE CAMPUS
ADDISON
SIMMONS

ANITA BOUTELL

DEATH BRINGS
A STORKE

CRADLED
IN FEAR

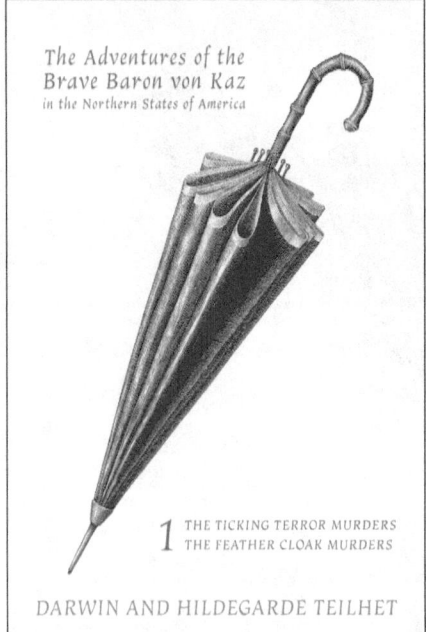

The Adventures of the
Brave Baron von Kaz
in the Northern States of America

1 THE TICKING TERROR MURDERS
THE FEATHER CLOAK MURDERS

DARWIN AND HILDEGARDE TEILHET

THE
DARTMOUTH
MURDERS

THE
WAILING ROCK
MURDERS

CLIFFORD
ORR

Coachwhip Publications
CoachwhipBooks.com

THE CASE OF THE
ADVERTISED
MURDER

MINNA BARDON

THE CRIME,
THE PLACE,
AND THE GIRL

DOUGLAS AND
DOROTHY STAPLETON

THE HOUSE THAT
JACK BUILT

with, MURDER IN AMBER

COLVER HARRIS

THE
DEATH
OF A
CELEBRITY

HULBERT
FOOTNER

AN AMOS LEE MAPPIN MYSTERY

Coachwhip Publications
CoachwhipBooks.com

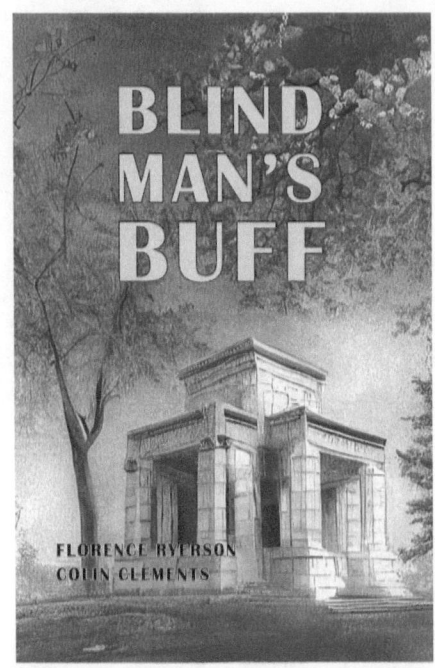

Coachwhip Publications
CoachwhipBooks.com

SAMUEL ROGERS

YOU'LL BE
SORRY!

YOU LEAVE
ME COLD!

Scarecrow
EATON K. GOLDTHWAITE

THE
13th
GUEST
by
ARMITAGE
TRAIL

THE JINX
THEATRE
MURDER

ALEXANDER WILLIAMS

Coachwhip Publications
CoachwhipBooks.com

THE SERGEANT HARTY MYSTERIES
JOEL Y. DANE

MURDER CUM LAUDE
1
THE CABANA MURDERS

FEAR
CAME
FIRST

VERA KELSEY

MAUDE PARKER

MURDER IN
JACKSON HOLE

MURDER ENDS
THE SONG

ALFRED MEYERS

Coachwhip Publications
CoachwhipBooks.com

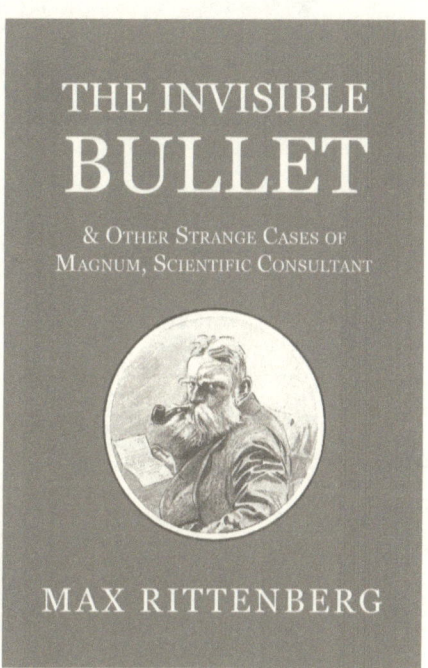
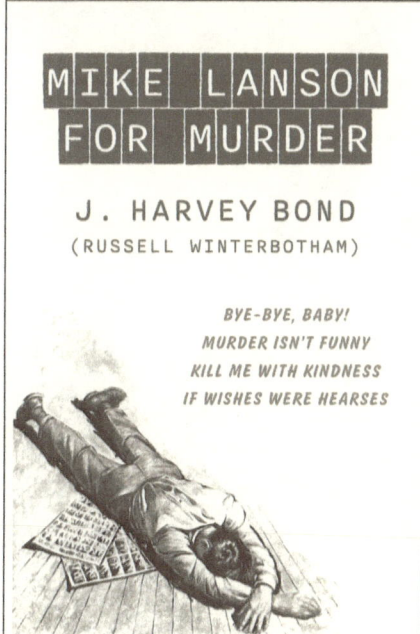

www.ingramcontent.com/pod-product-compliance
Lightning Source LLC
Chambersburg PA
CBHW020836260626
47169CB00003B/1014